A cursed witch unable to use her powers. A shifter who's lived this long by keeping to himself. A choice to save her—or himself.

Circe is a witch. Everyone says so. Her powers have yet to manifest, but even if they did, an ancient curse prohibits her from using them. She's also an orphan, and the coven that raised her reminds her of both every day. Lest she fall in love and very bad things will follow.

Yearning for a break from the coven's rituals and meddling, Circe strikes out on her own in Havenwood Falls, far away from the constant reminders that someone wants her blood.

Evan is that someone. He's a shifter—a truth he's hidden his entire existence, and the single reason a council of mages hired him. And now, thanks to an unfortunate and binding deal, Evan has been charged with locating Circe. He should have dealt with her ages ago, but he keeps finding excuses not to. And it's not only that he doesn't trust the council's motives, or that he has no interest in kidnapping an innocent girl.

This job is all he needs to resolve his bargain, yet Evan can't seem to follow through.

When the council tires of waiting, they take matters into their own hands. And Evan must decide: step out of the shadows to save her, or keep his own skin.

HAVENWOOD FALLS BOOKS

Forget You Not by Kristie Cook

Old Wounds by Susan Burdorf

Fate, Love & Loyalty by E.J. Fechenda

The Winged & the Wicked by T.V. Hahn & Kristie Cook

Alpha's Queen by Lila Felix

Ink & Fire by R.K. Ryals

Lose You Not by Kristie Cook

Tragic Ink by Heather Hildenbrand

Nowhere to Hide by Belinda Boring

Flames Among the Frost by Amy Hale

Rock Me Gently by Susan Burdorf

From the Embers by Amy Miles

Defying Gravity by Kallie Ross

Break Me Not by Kristie Cook

How the Dead Lie by Stacey Rourke

The Lurkers Within by Danielle Bannister

The Collector: Awakening by Kristie Cook, R.K. Ryals, Belinda Boring & Nadirah Foxx

Addicted to You by Belinda Boring

Affliction Mine by C.J. Pinard

The Ward & the Wanderers by T.V. Hahn

Toil & Trouble by Melissa Wright

Of Salt and Stars by Seven Jane

Redefined by Morgan Wylie

Betrayal Among the Frost by Amy Hale

Forever Loyal by E.J. Fechenda

Fate's Demand by Emily Cyr

The Wu & the Wand by T.V. Hahn

A Demon's Redemption by JD Nelson

Also try the YA line, Havenwood Falls High; the historical paranormal line, Legends of Havenwood Falls; the darker, sexier side of town, Havenwood Falls Sin & Silk; and the local supernatural college, Sun & Moon Academy.

Stay up to date at www.HavenwoodFalls.com

TOIL & TROUBLE

A HAVENWOOD FALLS NOVELLA

MELISSA WRIGHT

Double, double toil and trouble;
Fire burn, and cauldron bubble.
—William Shakespeare, *Macbeth*

PROLOGUE

He was supposed to take her. He hadn't. Five weeks and he hadn't. And now she'd gone into hiding, in a secret town nestled in the mountains of Colorado. Havenwood Falls: a haven for supernaturals. A place where she could have stayed safe indefinitely, if only he hadn't followed her.

He was a fool.

CHAPTER 1

*C*irce was cursed. Alone. And that was the way she liked it. Love was for fools, not someone like her. She had better things to do, she thought as she shoved her dirty clothes into two machines at the back of the local laundromat. She'd spent most of her life not needing to remind herself of the ancient edicts holding her magic and love life for ransom, but after a few days in Havenwood Falls, suddenly she was surrounded by shifters and supes with Adonis bodies and secret, sexy-times smiles. It was getting hard to stay focused.

A shifter of some sort leaned against the machine beside her, his thick arms flexing as they crossed over his chest. She couldn't tell what kind, but he radiated otherness, and everything about him tried to draw her in. She reached up to amp the volume on her earbuds and slammed the door on the washing machine a little too hard. *Fools*, she reminded herself. *Love is for fools.*

And dirty sexy-time was how you got there.

Laundry Playlist blaring in her ears, Circe turned to go. She'd grab coffee while she waited on the wash; that would at least get her away from the half-dressed blond who liked to practice stretching his quads during the spin cycle.

The apartment she'd moved into at Havenwood Village wasn't quite ready when she'd arrived, but if she could only hang on a few more days, she would finally be able to close herself in and introvert the hell out of it. As it was, a nice man from McCabe & Sons was banging and hammering around four or five hours a day to whittle down the extensive list of damages left by the previous occupant. Whatever had happened there hadn't been an easy thing. Circe couldn't be sure if it'd been caused by one supe or two, but signs pointed to a violent and unintentional shift in the center of a crowded apartment—and it hadn't gone well. Being exposed to new species was turning out to be a good reminder to Circe to be grateful for what she had—at least her magic wouldn't tear her apart.

She strolled down the sidewalk toward Coffee Haven, tugging her new puffer jacket tight around herself. She wouldn't miss the soul-scorching heat of an Arizona summer, but this "cool mountain breeze," as her new hosts had called it, was a pretty harsh swing. Piles of snow edged the town where the streets and sidewalks had been cleared, and Circe imagined there would be long stretches of winter where she did not even leave her home. Havenwood Falls had something else that desert town didn't have: a hefty population of supernatural beings.

Thanks to a nasty curse, Circe's mother had died during childbirth, leaving Circe orphaned. Well, that hadn't exactly been what had orphaned her. Circe had been told that once her mother was gone, her father couldn't stand to look at the child they'd created. He'd apparently abandoned Circe, left her on the steps of on old church inhabited by witches. Circe might have understood if he was too distraught to deal, but it was kind of hard to forgive something like that. Even now that the passage of time had given her distance from it.

Her father had dumped her, simple as that, and Circe had been left with nothing but a hand-me-down hex and a bad outlook.

So the witches who raised her became her guardians, and she counted the days until she was finally old enough to look out for herself. They'd insisted she call them all aunts, and she did love them, but some days they felt a lot more like jailers than kin. She'd played in the courtyard behind the church as a child, locked inside by invisible wards. The aunts had attempted a few play dates, but it was hard to find children who fit into a world so filled with magic, who would play among the church's crypts and lofts. So the cats and crows became her only friends.

She didn't know her birthday, but Circe had watched the calendar since she was big enough to read, and every March during the spring equinox ritual, she'd mark another year's passing. Eighteen of those ceremonies had come and gone without freedom.

And then, only weeks ago, a distant relative of one of the aunts had come for a visit. Lyra Beaumont had been pretty and petite, and pale enough it was clear she'd not lived through a recent Arizona summer. The aunts had met privately with her for long hours, and then they'd brought Circe in to be introduced. Circe had stood frozen in front of Lyra where she sat in a plush velvet chair, and it was gently explained that Circe would finally be allowed to leave their home.

Her heart was in her throat, but she still heard the truth of it. The offer came with a condition: she would be trading one set of wards for another. Circe could leave the coven, choose her own vocation, and live a real life, but only if she would come to Havenwood Falls, a place where she and her secrets could be protected. Lyra and the Beaumont family were apparently locals and members of the Luna Coven. Their coven and the governing body of the town—the Court of the Sun and the Moon—had been told of Circe's curse and her unusual situation.

The problem with not having a family is that you've got no one to ask what the hell you are. Circe's father had left her when she'd been no more than a baby. The aunts had found out what they could about him, and about Circe's curse, but it wasn't much. No one could be certain what might happen in her future.

Sure, the aunts had given her shelter until she reached an age where she could legally go out on her own—and even longer. They'd shown her what not to do. They'd shown her who to stay away from. They'd warned her of the curse, that she could never fall for a man or she would be doomed worse than her mother. But aside from that, aside from the constant assurances that she was a witch and that was all that mattered, they'd no idea where Circe really came from—what sort of beings her parents were. Circe knew she wasn't part shifter or vamp like some of the locals here. Not fae. But even though she hadn't come into her full power, something potent was inside of her. She felt it—the magic that ran through her blood, strong and dangerous.

Capable of decimating the shadows that followed her.

And, unlike the aunts, Lyra and her coven were not keeping Circe tucked away.

A chime dinged on the street in front of her, the door to Shelf Indulgence opening as a tall brunette came out. The woman smelled of herbs and tonics, and something like home. Circe didn't want to go back, but it was hard not to miss a place she'd been for nineteen years. Circe smiled, and the woman gave her a friendly wave, fumbling her books and packages before regaining control. One door down, and Circe was at Coffee Haven, near the center of a line of shops that faced the town square.

It was lovely inside, with worn hardwood floors and a long marble counter like an old-fashioned ice cream parlor. The walls were covered in art, hanging plants and crystals were scattered around the space, and Circe was comfortable despite the press of the crowd. She leaned against the counter, deciding on a sweet orange tea before being talked into a blueberry scone by a petite blonde whose name tag read "Willow." Circe had encountered the woman the previous day and noticed she seemed exceptionally good at reading people, that she had an uncanny intuition. There was a sense of otherness about this Willow, and Circe wondered if she had empathic abilities. Circe had been a bundle of nerves that first day, and Willow had immediately offered a selection of calming teas and sweet cakes.

Circe had liked her right away.

Today, Circe took her purchases to a small table against the wall and was immediately glad she chose the scone. Her gaze wandered over the crowd, taking in a myriad of supernatural tells and what appeared to be simply normal human beings, all going about their lives as if this wasn't an entirely epic event. Circe being alone. On her own. Thoroughly without the watching eyes of her many, many aunts.

Her gaze trailed over the wall of art, pencils and acrylics and oils, all varied in style and skill, and she realized they must have been the work of local artists. Her stomach dipped at the idea of the possibility, and she added it to the growing list of potential thrills: someday seeing her own watercolors on display. In public. She caught herself grinning like an idiot and bit the edge of her lip against that grin. Didn't want the residents of Havenwood Falls to think she was one of *those* witches.

And then a shadow moved at the edge of the storefront window outside, and Circe's mood fell. She wasn't under the watchful eye of the coven, but that didn't mean she was alone.

It didn't mean she was safe.

Circe grimaced, keeping her head down as she finished her

scone. The tea was sweet, with just a little bite, and it warmed her all the way through. She thought she was brave enough now for her meeting with Addie, so she picked up her handbag overstuffed with elixirs and charms thanks to the vigilant aunts, and left the safety of Coffee Haven to tick off one more task.

Adelaide Beaumont, youngest of the Beaumont witches and Lyra's daughter, was not what Circe had expected. The aunts had called her a business manager and court liaison, but here she was in a hoodie and ripped jeans, legs crossed at the ankles with a worn pair of Chuck Taylor All Stars propped on the edge of the desk.

She snapped her gum, sitting up to give Circe a knowing smile as she spotted her in the doorway.

"Do I look that nervous?" Circe asked.

Addie chuckled. "It'll be over in a jiffy."

Circe managed to smile back as she looked at the woman, searching for signs of familiarity. Addie was a Beaumont too, which meant she was some distant relative of Morgan, one of the many "aunts." Morgan had never specified the exact relationship, but it was apparently close enough that the Beaumonts would do her this favor, that they would allow Circe a safe haven even knowing she would soon develop dangerous powers.

Circe cleared her throat. In truth, it wasn't the needle she was afraid of. "So this is permanent?"

Addie glanced up from the supplies she was laying out on the table, her wrists layered in bracelets and stones. She cocked a brow behind her black-framed glasses. "Already planning on running away?"

Circe took a deep breath and stepped forward. "No, I'm here for good."

She reached a hand out to Addie, cementing her independence from the aunts, committing her soul to Havenwood Falls.

CHAPTER 2

*E*van followed her as she walked alone through the town, apparently unaware of the danger she was in. Circe Alexander—nineteen years old, five foot four, brown hair, brown eyes, no identifiable markings—had been under the protection of thirteen women since the moment he'd found her, and now suddenly she was strolling around on her own, like she didn't have a care in the world. She'd been doing laundry, having coffee, browsing books, and now it looked as if she was sporting a brand new tattoo. So much for no identifiable markings. It was utterly baffling. And yet, here he was, watching her still.

Tattoo still fresh and pink, Circe sauntered along the town square, rubbing her hands and blowing a breath to warm them. It wasn't overly cold, but she was a transplant, and that made all the difference. Evan wore a jacket over his henley, but only so he could turn up the collar in an effort to blend in. The magic in his blood kept him warm enough, and the jacket had done little to keep him under the radar. This was a town scattered with supernaturals. They could sense their own. They knew he was something different.

Nothing about this bargain was going the right way, and every fiber of Evan's being told him to run. But Evan couldn't run. He'd made a deal. The thing about deals with mages is that they're unaccountably binding. Impossible to break. And, more often than not, started and ended in blood.

Evan ran a finger over the scar at the base of his thumb. He'd been desperate when he'd sought out the mages, desperate enough he hadn't thought about how dangerous they were—and foolish enough to think his life could get no worse. And then they had marked him, ran a ritual dagger across his palm before he realized what they'd done. They had his blood.

They wanted hers.

Circe turned into the laundromat and a cat shifter—probably Evan's least favorite kind—held the door for her, leaning too close and giving Circe a pointed smile. She ducked her head and pressed the earbuds into her ears. Evan waited as she folded her clothes and tucked them into an oversized tote, tugged the straps onto her shoulder, and headed back for the door. She had one more stop: the vet's office, where she would be picking up what might have been the ugliest bulldog Evan had ever seen.

When she finally stepped out of Havenwood Falls Animal Hospital, Circe knelt beside the beast, cooing and babbling and carrying on about how wonderful he looked. "He's got the prettiest trimmed nails and the softest coat, and he's such a good boy." And then she kissed him. Full on, right over his big slobbery mouth. The dog smiled, or appeared to, his maw going wide and his tongue lolling out as he panted. Chompers, it seemed, was also not too cold in the mountain climate.

Circe appeared to suddenly realize she was kneeling on a public sidewalk, her recently washed tote of clothes in danger of spilling and her purse abandoned in her haste to lavish praise upon this dog. She gathered her bags onto her shoulder and gave Chompers one final *good boy* pat. He waddled to standing, following obediently on his purple-patterned leash. They walked down Petran Street the few blocks to her apartment, and Evan found an alcove on an adjacent building, settling in to watch the door.

His cell phone buzzed in his pocket, but he did not check the screen. He knew what it was going to say.

There were no more excuses, no more chances to buy time. He was going to have to do it. Tonight would be the night. The mages were on a deadline, and there was no way he could wait any longer and remain alive. It was her or him, and as much as it turned his stomach, Evan wasn't stupid. If he didn't hand her over, someone else would.

And they might not be as gentle about it.

He ran a palm over his face, thinking through his plan for the dozenth time. Second floor window, while she was asleep. Tainted rag over her mouth, band of herbs around her wrist. The mages had sent him with an arsenal of spelled weapons for one single woman. *She's dangerous*, Lucius had told him, the head of the powerful council taking the time to warn Evan himself. *Do not give her a chance.*

That was the thing that had stuck with Evan the most. The thing that had made him hesitate that first day. Dangerous, they'd said. A killer, no mercy, no code. Evan knew about witches. He'd had firsthand experience with the way they could destroy lives. He had been fully prepared to do what the council had asked, and then he'd seen her in the yard of the old church that housed the coven, and he'd wondered if that could ever be true. If Circe the witch could really be dangerous.

She had been reading in the morning sun, legs crossed over a blanket in the landscaped yard out back of the old church. One of their many cats sat beside her, preening until its black fur glistened like wet lacquer. Evan had watched as a small bird alighted on the stepping stones, not ten feet from that very cat. Circe's gaze had flicked to it, and the bird became hidden by a cloud of gray smoke until it lifted once more into the air. Spared from the keen eyes of the cat, just like that.

Dangerous. A killer. Eater of the hearts of men.

Savior of tiny birds.

Reader of historical fiction.

It wasn't as if Evan had trusted the mages to begin with, or even wanted to do their work, but when he made the bargain, he'd had no other choice. If he didn't do something, the magic inside of Evan would destroy him. He'd meant to gain freedom from a drawn-out, torturous destruction in exchange for completing a single task for them. Taking down a witch—a ruthless killer—seemed less an offense than stealing a harmless girl. So he'd waited. He'd watched her. That day, and the next. Nothing had ever changed in her, not even when under stress. Circe had never used magic again, aside from that first day, and Evan began to wonder if he'd seen it right at all. When she'd found herself in sticky situations with her guardians, when she'd been caught out in the rain, troubles large or small—never once did she reach for that power, never once did she use it to help herself or to hurt a soul.

Evan had made a bad bargain. He knew that much for sure. And now it was time to pay the piper.

Now, he was afraid, he was about to kidnap an innocent girl.

CHAPTER 3

*C*irce opened the door to her apartment just as the contractor was wiping his hands on an old strip of cloth. He tucked it into his back pocket and nodded in greeting. "Afternoon. Looks like we've got you all finished up."

Chompers jerked on his leash, pulling Circe closer so he could snuffle at the poor man's boots. Circe smiled up at him apologetically. Ryker, he'd said his name was. He was well over six feet tall and built of muscle. His blond hair was pulled back while he worked, his blue eyes bright. When Circe was this close to a man who seemed capable of snapping a person in two, she couldn't help but think of the aunts' warnings. But while Ryker was certainly dangerous, he didn't actually make Circe feel scared.

"Thank you so much," she said. "For everything." She took a cursory glance around the apartment. "It looks great."

It did, really. It was barely decorated, but what was there was hers. The apartment might have been small, but it felt like Circe, and it felt like home.

He picked up his tool bag and tipped his hat. "It's nothing. Sorry you had to wait." He turned at the door, and as Circe bent to unsnap Chompers's leash, he added, "Don't forget to lock up behind me. Better safe than sorry, you know."

"Yes," Circe said, ignoring the chill that ran over her skin. "I'll be sure to remember."

The latch clicked as he closed the door behind him, and Circe moved to lock both the deadbolt and chain, and then check the windows. She'd not heard of any break-ins in the community, but common criminals weren't what she was worried about keeping out.

"Right," she told herself. "Back to the old bag of tricks."

She moved down the short hallway to the kitchenette, opening the pantry that held her stock. The aunts had made her promise to set wards, and she supposed now that she was truly alone, she should do at least that much. She took down the bottles and jars, and though they were unlabeled, she knew what was in each and every one. She felt silly singing with no one else in the apartment, so she hummed the tune and mumbled the words where they needed to strike. She was eager to heat up water for tea, but that would have to wait. It was never a good idea to mix cooking with casting.

Circe thought about her afternoon while she worked, specifically her visit to the Havenwood Falls Animal Hospital. One of her aunts had secured her a position there as a groomer and after her meeting with the owner, Isa Hilton, Circe had never felt better about the prospect of a job that would be fulfilling, something she actually enjoyed and could be proud of. It might not be the job she'd always dreamed of, but it was working with animals, and Circe had always been good at that. She knew it was something that made her happy. Something that might start to heal the empty place inside her. For now, she didn't have the required degree to become a vet tech, but the beauty of Havenwood Falls was that so many of its residents were like Circe. It would give her the opportunity to use her gifts to help in those special circumstances, licensed or not, when it was a risk to ask those who were not *in the know* for help.

While the veterinarian owner, Isa, was human, it was clear there was something supernatural within her, and she too was aware of the mixed population of the Havenwood Falls community. Isa was slim and lovely, and just the tiniest bit terrifying, but she'd fallen into easy conversation with Circe once they'd taken a short tour around the animal hospital and the adjacent shelter. Isa had a few volunteers, but the shelter was woefully understaffed, so Circe hoped she'd be able to spend a few extra hours there as well.

She smiled at the memory of the petite redheaded volunteer— probably only a year or so younger than Circe—who had arrived wearing rubber boots and shorts, when Circe herself had been freezing.

She sprinkled her ingredients into the mortar and ground them into a fine dust as Chompers slurped huge gulps of water, spilling and sloshing it out of his bowl beside her.

"Good thing the kitchen floors are laminate in this place," she told the dog.

He smiled up at her with a row of crooked teeth, then ambled off to find his bed. She couldn't help but laugh whenever he walked away, knowing exactly how he would trot toward his padded cushion, circle three times, and then flop down, legs akimbo. If Circe was ever in danger of loving anything too much, it was that dog.

She returned to the front door, singing the required words as she dusted a few pinches of the concoction at its threshold. She did the same for the bedroom window, and then crossed to the living room to dust that sill as well.

When she leaned forward, mouth pursed to form the words, fingers outstretched with a pinch of powder, something launched through the glass.

Circe's back hit the hardwood floor of the living room, wind knocked out of her, and she had the faint realization that there had been no glass. The window had been open, not broken, and the high winds and cold mountain air hadn't moved through it to alert her. She had just checked it.

But she couldn't think of that. She could only struggle for breath as the large form on top of her crushed her chest. He was reaching for her face, struggling against her to smear something sickly sweet on her skin while Chompers wrestled with his leg.

The large man was cursing, she thought, in some foreign language, and his magic felt *off*. The skin of his arm was cold and bristly beneath her hands as she tried to push him away. She'd left her potions on the counter, her knife right along with them. Such a stupid, stupid mistake. She'd only been here a matter of days, and they'd already found her. Had her pinned to the floor. Chompers growled and bit, but the man didn't let go to knock the dog back. He kept pressing down on her, trying to cover her face with that stinking rag. He clambered for a better grip on her, pressing knees and elbows hard into her limbs, and the weight of him was too much for Circe to push off or wiggle out of. The aunts had taught her self-defense, though, and they were not above fighting dirty.

Circe's full powers hadn't manifested, so she couldn't change a being's actual makeup, but she could create illusions. She pressed her palms to the floor beneath her, willing the wood to look like a chasm, like the sharp edge of a cliff, hundreds of feet down. Like the man was falling. She saw the moment he noticed, and even if he'd been warned she might fool him, it was the hesitation she needed. She called to the dust left on her fingers and used it to transform the shape of the bracelet wrapping her wrist into a crude knife. She didn't have the right ingredients, hadn't given it the proper time, but she didn't need the spell to stick long. She only needed a second to use it as a weapon before it fell back into the shape it truly was.

Circe gripped the lumpy blade in her fist and struck hard and fast at the man's ribs.

But the man had disappeared.

Suddenly, and quite unexpectedly, the hulking figure that had pinned her down was gone. Her makeshift blade stuck out of the side of someone else. Someone smaller and less beastly than her attacker.

Circe blinked, stunned, and the stabbed man stared back at her, just as shocked.

"You," she hissed.

And then the large man she'd intended to stab instead struck this new one in the face. Chompers leapt at the large man, tearing his dark pants to shreds, and Circe remembered herself. She picked up the lamp from the side table and smashed it into her attacker's head as he fought with the other man. The lamp cord jerked where it was attached to the wall, and Circe came off balance, holding the wire framework as shattered bits fell. The man she'd stabbed rammed into the bulky one, and both slammed into her newly repaired living room wall. The stabbed man reached into his jacket pocket, drew out a small square of cloth, and pressed it over the bulky man's mouth and nose. There was a short struggle as Circe looked on, bewildered, and then the bulky man seemed to fall asleep.

Circe's hands were trembling. She realized she was still holding parts of the busted lamp. The man she'd stabbed slumped against the wall beside his victim, blood dampening his side where her blade had been. It was on the floor now, once more a thick round bangle, sprinkled with blood.

The bracelet smelled strongly of magic and something earthy. And maybe some fur.

Circe stood there for far longer than she was proud of before she remembered to take some sort of action. She scrambled into the kitchen, grabbed her athame from the counter, and ran back to the living area. Chompers and the man she'd stabbed stared at her. She aimed the considerably more dangerous knife at the stabbed man, and Chompers took over watching the man who'd passed out. He was big on teamwork, that dog.

"What are you doing?" Circe hissed at the stabbed man.

He gaped at her, like maybe he had *no idea* what he was doing. And certainly that he'd not expected for it to end like this. His hand was pressed to his side, blood seeping slowly between his fingers. Circe cursed, then said sorry, because she didn't think it was polite to swear in front of guests, no matter what the witches who raised her said.

The man seemed to think she was apologizing for stabbing him, which she most definitely was not. He said, "It's not deep. I should be fine soon."

His voice said otherwise, though, and Circe could see he was in pain. She pursed her lips, considering her options.

"What are you going to do?" she asked the stabbed man.

"I'll stitch it up, I guess—"

The look she gave cut him off. "About me. About him."

She gestured toward the other man with the tip of her blade.

"No," the stabbed man said. "We aren't together. I was—I was trying to stop him. Didn't you see?"

She crossed her arms, keeping the knife securely in her fist. "I see all right. I see you every day, following me like I'm too slow to notice. I see you lurking around every corner and keeping track of everything I do. I see that you've got potions on you that were made by a skilled hand, and I know that hand wasn't yours." He opened his mouth to speak, and just to be sure he understood she'd meant he wasn't a witch, that she could sense the shifter on him, she snapped, "You smell like dog."

He looked hurt. Like, genuinely offended.

"So," she said. "What are you going to do?"

He closed his eyes, shook his head slowly. When he looked at her again, all the energy seemed to drain out of him. "I'm not going to do anything. I didn't lie—he's not with me. He's my replacement. If they've sent him, then it wouldn't matter if I handed you to them right now. I'm already a marked man."

She nodded. It was probably what he deserved.

"And what about him?" She gestured again toward the other man.

"What do you mean?"

"Well, *do* something with him."

His expression said, *like what?*

"I don't want him in here. This is my home. It's brand new, and I prefer it without some random shifter passed out in the middle of my floor. Can you understand that?"

She was, admittedly, a little on edge after being attacked.

The stabbed man struggled to his feet. "I'm sorry, Circe. What would you have me do with him?"

She swallowed hard, staggered by his casual use of her name. Like they knew each other. Like they were friends. But he did know her, didn't he? The same way she'd gotten to know him. He'd been following her for weeks.

"Just get rid of him," she snapped. "Out the window."

The stabbed man stared at her.

She sighed. "He's got magic in his blood. It won't kill him. And if he gets a few broken bones, it's no more than he asked for."

"Are you not concerned what the neighbors might think?"

"You throw him out," she said. "I'll do the rest."

CHAPTER 4

*E*van watched as the woman he'd been following for weeks and weeks without doing magic turned a man into a shapeless lump of fur. She'd drawn a small vial of green powder out of her purse, spread it on her fingers, spat on each of her hands, and then pressed her palms to the man's skin. She was humming and singing something too low for him to make out the words, and the dirty brown fur morphed into a thing decidedly more solid.

"A coyote?"

She didn't look at him when she replied, because despite the fact that he'd just saved her, Circe wasn't as helpless and fragile as she'd seemed. She wasn't worried about turning her back on a man.

"Less suspicious if someone sees it outside," she said. "I might have used a dog, but I can't stand the sight of one looking hurt." She smiled at Chompers, who watched with something like approval in his dark eyes. "Okay." She stood, brushing her hands clean on her jeans. "He's still pretty heavy. I didn't change his true form; it's just a temporary illusion."

She gestured toward the window, and though he couldn't believe he was actually doing it, Evan picked up a man who was a coyote and threw him out the opening of the second-story apartment.

They both leaned over the sill to watch him land. They both winced when he did.

Evan pressed a hand to his side as he straightened up. Circe was right; the coyote had still been man-weight. He felt a little light-headed and leaned against the wall.

"Sit down," she said. "I'll make something for your side."

"I should go," he started, but Circe cut him off.

"What you should do is sit down. I have to call the Court of the Sun and the Moon to report this . . . coyote attack." She slid the window shut and moved to the kitchen to retrieve her stone mortar. "If someone has truly marked you, you'll have no chance to defend yourself in your condition." She sprinkled something from the bowl onto the window sill, whispering words beneath her breath. "I'll help you with that and then . . . we'll see."

And then she can use me as bait? Evan thought. *Dangle me out her window so she can catch her next attacker?* He swayed, and Circe grabbed Evan's arm to help him to a seat. He flopped hard onto a couch covered in throw pillows and overstuffed cushions, and Circe made him move his hand so she could see the wound. He didn't look at his side, but he saw her face.

He had the feeling she didn't like touching him.

He remembered he was her enemy.

He closed his eyes, knowing she could plant her knife in his exposed belly anytime she wanted. It would maybe be a better way to go than whatever the council of mages had planned.

"Hey," Circe snapped.

He blinked his eyes open, then wondered if he'd missed a moment or two. He'd lost time like that before, while the magic in his blood stitched him back together. Circe was wiping her hands on a white dish towel.

"Try to stay awake. I've got water on the boil. The remedy will take a few minutes to steep before I can use it." She pointed a thumb over her shoulder. "I'm going to take a quick shower. Don't answer the door. Don't try to leave."

Evan nodded, or at least thought he did, before his eyes were closed again. He heard shuffling noises, the muffled click of a door latch, and voices fading in and out. Circe, calling to report her attacker's body outside. What had she said? The Court of the Sun and the Moon? Evan wondered why she had waited, why she'd not immediately called for help. She'd had him at knifepoint, and the other man had been knocked out, so what was she planning?

And then he lost more time to sleep. When he finally came to, Circe was leaning over him, brows knit as she examined his wound. Her hair was damp, twisted into a knot over one shoulder. She wore a thin white T-shirt over black leggings. She was at ease enough to dress comfortably—that was something at least. Not that he could do much in the way of attacking her at the moment, even if he wanted to. His side ached, and his head felt as if he was in a fog.

Something cold pressed his skin, and he winced.

"There," Circe said. "That should do it."

She glanced up at him. Her eyes were cognac. He hadn't seen them this close before; he'd thought they were chestnut, like her hair.

"I put about five stitches in. It wasn't a wide cut, so you could have gotten by with less, but this will heal more cleanly."

She brushed a strand of hair away from her face. She had a set of stacked silver rings on her first finger, a small dark mark across her third. Her nails were short, cut clean, and polished shiny black. She usually wore pink, he thought.

Circe frowned at him, and he realized he'd said the thought out loud.

"Evan—" she started.

He pushed up from the couch. Or he intended to. He couldn't seem to get his limbs to work right. How did she know his name? It wasn't that she'd gone through his wallet. That ID said David Jackson, Casper, Wyoming. His throat was dry, his hands all itchy.

"What did you give me?"

His accusation fell flat, and Circe was not surprised. "Just something to help you let down your guard. It'll wear off soon."

"You drugged me to ask me questions?"

She crossed her arms over her chest. "Yes. And you broke into my apartment after stalking me for weeks."

She was so small, her face so soft and sweet. All he'd ever seen her be was kind. He couldn't believe she'd done this.

He couldn't believe after all this time, after wallowing in guilt over what he was going to have to do to her, that he actually felt betrayed.

"Give me the antidote."

Circe shrugged. "It doesn't matter now. You've told me what I needed to hear."

She walked toward the kitchen, and Evan watched her go. And he kept watching her. And he remembered something else about witches, something about how they could beguile and seduce. How the illusions were not just for changing men into beasts.

"What do you look like?" he asked her. "Really?" Under all that trickery, he meant. Beneath that face that couldn't be real.

She barked a laugh, returning to the living room with a mug in each hand.

"You think I'd turn myself into this? Evan, come on. I'd at least make myself tall." There was something in her tone that was off, though; something that said his question made her uncomfortable. She lifted a bare foot to press his legs over and sat on the edge of the couch next to him. "Besides, you're one to talk."

MELISSA WRIGHT

She handed him a mug of what appeared to be hot tea. It did not smell half so pleasant. "Here, drink this."

He narrowed his eyes on her.

"You wanted the antidote. You don't have to drink it." She started to take the glass away, but he brought it to his lips.

It was hot, and it smelled like road tar. He gulped it down anyway, desperate to be rid of whatever was fogging his head. It worked immediately, then he wanted to retch. She moved a plastic trash bin closer to him, then handed him the other mug.

"This one's tea. It will get rid of that terrible taste, but it's mostly just yarrow and peppermint to soothe your stomach."

She returned to the kitchen, humming something quietly as Evan leaned over the waste bin. He could hear her open the fridge, the click of a gas stove, and then a cast iron griddle sliding against its racks. He closed his eyes and breathed, catching the scent of peppermint and spice. It was soon replaced with seared steak, and at the sound of clattering dishes, Evan pushed himself to sitting. He didn't know if he could eat, but she'd gone to the trouble, and now that his head was clearing, he remembered he was technically in the wrong here. Although she *had* stabbed him, it had been an accident. The utter shock on her face couldn't have been faked, even by a woman he'd seen change a man into a canine.

She came back into the room, grinning a ridiculously out-of-place grin, and Evan was taken aback, again, at the change in her up close. There was something startling about her, something he couldn't seem to take his eyes off for long. He searched for what he might say to her when she'd bring him the plate, what words he could give her to reassure, or to say thanks. He wasn't certain what he owed her, but Evan wanted nothing more than to be in her good graces. He thought of the man outside the window. He did not want to be one of *them*. Not someone who worked for the mages who wanted her brought in.

24

He leaned forward to receive the plate, only to watch Circe walk right past him. She sat the plate on the floor and let out a long string of cooing, burbling *good boys*. Her smile fell as Chompers took to the steak, and she glanced at Evan. His expression must have been something to behold. She laughed.

"Oh, you thought that was for you? Well, you can ask. Maybe he'll share."

Evan shook his head. "He deserves it."

Circe put her hands on her knees and pushed to standing. "He does. He's a good dog."

"Ugly but loyal?" Evan mused.

Circe narrowed her gaze on Evan, though he was pretty sure she knew the comment was only meant in jest. "Don't let him hear that. He has his heart set on something big. Maybe becoming a model one day." Her brow waggled. "Or a mascot."

"A mascot for what?"

She shrugged a shoulder. "A hotdog company, most likely. The boy likes to eat."

Evan laughed, even if it was half-hearted. And then he froze.

"What?" Circe asked.

"He is really a dog, though, isn't he?"

CHAPTER 5

*C*irce gave Evan her worst scowl. "Of course he's a dog. What is wrong with you?"

Evan raised one shoulder. "I don't know. I mean, there is a coyote on the ground outside who used to be something else. Maybe this bulldog used to be your mailman."

She looked at him for a minute, knowing her guilt over the coyote-man was stamped on her face, and said, "He's not there anymore. I called the Court of the Sun and the Moon. They came to get him." She sighed. "He was attacking me. It's not like I had much choice."

Evan was thoughtful for an equal measure of time. Circe wished she could read minds, but what he'd said when she'd drugged him to work on his side made things clear enough. She took a sip from her mug to hide her blush. She would *not* think of those things now, not with him inches away on her sofa.

"Why didn't you just call them then?" Evan asked. "He was incapacitated, and you had me under threat of your knife. Why wait?"

"I don't know," she answered. "I just . . . I wanted to be able to do this on my own."

She'd thought about that over and over when she'd locked herself in her new bathroom to take a shower. What was she doing? Why was she keeping him safe? She didn't have a good answer. She'd been covered in dog slobber and the scent of that strange, horrible man. She'd just needed a shower. She'd just needed to think things through. And now it had been hours, and she'd spoken with the Court and not mentioned Evan. She'd made herself tea, and here she was, still not letting this man go. His wounds weren't that bad. They would heal. Besides, he'd been planning to kidnap her for some horrible council, so what if they did catch him? Circe had not meant to stab him. It had been an accident; it hadn't filled her with guilt. That was not what was eating at her. What really bothered her was that he'd been trying to save her.

It was not what bad men were supposed to do.

It was not what he'd been hired for. Not the thing he'd signed his life away over, risked it all with that thin scar at the base of his thumb.

Circe shivered, glancing at the closed curtains hiding the window the man had come through.

Evan noticed. "So you know you aren't safe here. What are you going to do?"

"I am safe here," she said stubbornly. "The town has wards. I have protections, my spells. There are people here to help me if I need it."

"They know how to get past the wards. And you're here alone. If you can't get to a phone or—"

She frowned. Obviously both Evan and the other man had somehow gotten past the town's wards. And she'd not set her own protections in place at that cursed window, even though she knew at the very least Evan had been out there. She'd gotten complacent. She'd trusted her stalker.

But he had come to her rescue. She hadn't been wrong.

"How can you act like you're so worried about it? You were going to kidnap me for some shady council of mages."

Evan looked like he'd been slapped. She'd gotten the information dishonestly, but that didn't make it any less true. Even if he hadn't acted on it, Evan had known she was in danger. He'd not been watching her to keep her safe. He'd been watching her for them. He'd not acted himself until the last possible moment.

"I didn't have a choice," he said.

Circe believed him. He'd said as much when he'd been talking in his stupor. The magic in his blood was going to kill him. There was something she didn't know, though. "Why?"

His eyes met hers, soft and hazel, and Circe let herself really look at him. His hair was sandy, a shade darker at the roots. It was a little too long on top and looked like maybe he'd been cutting it himself. His jaw was square and a bit stubbly, and his lips . . . Circe drew a sharp breath, snapped her eyes back to his. Gods, why was she staring at his mouth? What was *wrong* with her?

Evan drew a breath of his own, long and deep. Full of hopelessness or regret, she couldn't be sure. "I was hexed. Years ago. I was hanging out with some friends—somewhere I shouldn't have been. One of them was mixed up with a supernatural—a fae, I think. I was so young. I didn't even understand the strangeness about him. Didn't know this other world existed. But I paid for it anyway. We all did. There were four of us, and only one of him. We didn't think it would be . . . well, we just didn't think. We stood up for our friend, puffed up our chests, and jumped in on his side. But there was some sort of payment, I guess, some debt owed, and when the witch came to collect from that fae, we were no more than flies as far as she was concerned. She snapped her fingers, and the friend beside me went down. I tried to help him, but I didn't know what she'd done. It took two more before I realized what was happening."

Evan shook his head. "When I leapt for her, she just looked at me, her eyes as black as pitch. The corner of her mouth went down, barely a grimace, and I slammed into the ground. The hex tore through me, like swords of ice."

Evan drew a shuddering breath, looked back to Circe. "She turned me. Used me to dispatch that fae. Guess she didn't want to get her hands dirty." At Circe's expression, Evan added, "She's gone now, killed by some fool she'd set another hex on. The guy thought he was going to fix her, that he was so cunning he could best a thousand-year-old sorceress. He had no idea he was dooming us to stay like this for eternity. No one has been able to help us. No one has figured out how to undo what she has done."

"You're a shifter?"

"Yes, but not like the ones you might have met. I wasn't born this way, Circe. My change is not tied to the moon. I don't have a pack. It's just me, and this hex, and whatever other poor souls like me that are out there trying to find a way to live."

Circe shivered each time Evan spoke her name. She curled her arms around a pillow, drew it in against her chest. He'd spoken some about that other man in his mutterings. About how the magic inside him would not let him die, even as it slowly ate at him. He had tried again and again to end the suffering, and it had driven him half insane. She understood why now. She hoped Evan had never been that desperate.

And then she realized he had.

"That's why you made a deal with the mages. To get out from under your hex."

Evan nodded. "They told me you were like her. That you were a witch who used men. Who turned them into beasts at your whim."

29

Circe's mouth went dry, and she felt a little sick. She was that woman. She was a horrible, horrible thing. What she did was transmogrification. The illusions came easier, yes, but only because she'd been doing that her entire life. Her true power would include the ability to change man into beast just as easily. It was brand new to her now—she was only just coming of age and developing that power—but if she were to live a thousand years, what sort of monstrous being would she become? The darkness was in her. Would she hex a man just to do it? Would she hurt someone for no valid reason?

Evan saw her expression, moved to touch her, then drew back as if in confusion.

"What will they do to you?" she asked him. He didn't answer. But Circe knew. They had taken his blood. His punishment would be worse than death. He'd only forfeited his life in that it now belonged to them. She swallowed hard and whispered, "What do they want with me?"

The aunts had told her she was in danger. Because of the curse. The curse that killed her mother. The curse that would be reborn the moment she fell in love. She didn't know why.

She'd been raised around magic, though. She understood that sometimes it truly was only a witch's whim. She knew there didn't need to be sound logic when the world was full of jealousy and spite.

Evan glanced down, and this time Circe knew it was shame. "I don't know. I made the agreement without even finding out why." He forced himself to look at her as he continued. "I thought you were like her. I thought it didn't matter why they needed you. I thought with one less witch, the world might be a better place."

His honesty cut her to the heart, but his words left open possibilities. His confession said that he was changed, that now he wasn't so sure. Circe wished she had the conviction to convince him she was worth saving. Or at least convince herself.

"Are you hungry?" she asked.

Evan might have been caught off guard by her sudden subject change, but he didn't let on. "No, I don't think I am." She wondered if his side was hurting him terribly, or if he had an ill feeling the way she did, thinking of hexes and curses and men shifting into beasts. He said, "I wouldn't mind another drink, though. Maybe something with just tea leaves and water this time?"

She managed a smile. "You'd be surprised what I can do with just leaves and water."

"I'm surprised by everything you do, Circe Alexander."

Circe felt her chest tighten, and she spun to make the short walk to the kitchen. She was in trouble, and she knew it. Evan didn't know about the terms of her curse, but she was one hundred percent aware. She could feel it in every bone of her body. She could feel him, too, like he was a lodestone. She was walking on dangerous ground.

The worst part was, it was maybe the most thrilling thing she'd ever done. The most *her* she'd ever felt.

She leaned behind a column to smack her forehead against the wall. "Circe," she muttered, "you are a bad, bad witch."

CHAPTER 6

*E*van was in trouble. This girl was going to be the end of him, he just knew it. They'd sat on her sofa, talking as the lights outside faded and the moon rose. They were talking still. About everything, and nothing. What he'd wanted to be as a child, what his favorite foods were. Circe kept asking, and Evan kept making excuses to himself. Surely, she needed him there. She'd been attacked earlier in the afternoon; some strange man had been inside her home. A home that was new to her. She was scared. She was lonely. He was obligated for what he'd done. But those things were far from the truth.

Circe was strong.

Circe was determined.

Evan was there because he could not make himself want to leave.

She'd been telling him about the witches who'd raised her, and he could hear the wistfulness in her voice. She missed them, even though leaving to start her own life was what she wanted more than anything else. She'd been orphaned, and everything about her life had been someone else's choice. Now she was here and determined to make it work.

She didn't bring up Evan's family, and for that he was grateful. He didn't like to think about the world he'd left behind. The memories he'd stored away. They were not sweet stories of bickering women and spells gone wrong. Not when a sorceress controlled your blood. Used you to kill.

Evan said, "And so the coven named you?"

She smirked. "Yes. After a mythological goddess who turned men into swine. 'Lest you forget men are pigs,' they like to remind me."

Evan remembered the goddess's story. It was a tale of isolation. "It's Greek, right?"

She nodded. "It means 'to secure with rings' or 'hoop around.' It's a reference to the binding power of magic." Her expression said, *Those witches, always thinking they're so clever.*

She sat her empty mug on the side table. "And Alexander is apparently from my mother's family. Since my father ran off and left me, the aunts refused to use his surname. They didn't like to talk about him at all. When I would finally wear them down with questions, I could tell they were filtering what they told me. It seemed like there were a lot of sidelong glances and clandestine conversations, and even though they are more than a little resourceful, they would only let on like they'd discovered a few small details."

She ran a thumb across the thin stacked bands on her finger as she considered. "I did some research once when I was younger, going through a bit of a rebellious phase. Breaking all the rules. I'd tried a tracking spell and a summoning spell and everything you can imagine, but what finally tipped me off with where to start was a scrap of paper in Anise's spellbook." She laughed, shook her head.

"It was something like Hallewell. Lucius Hallewell, maybe." She waved it off. "I don't remember for sure. His name led to nothing but dead ends, and eventually I got some hobbies that didn't involve research or boys."

Evan froze. Every fiber of his being wanted to shout the name back at her, to be certain that was what she'd said. But it was. He knew it in his soul.

It explained everything.

And if the witches she was so fond of hadn't told her . . . Evan worked to school his features.

"Do you trust them?" he said. "The witches in the coven that raised you? The aunts. They're worthy of your trust?" He was stumbling over his words, but Circe didn't seem to notice.

"Yeah," she said. "I mean, they're witches. They like to meddle in my business, and they're constantly doing rituals to try to change the fates . . ." She shook her head. "I trust them. They're ridiculous and mostly insufferable, but they're good at heart."

She must have mistaken his expression. She said, "Let me take a look at your wound."

He might have argued, said it would heal on its own, that that wasn't what had him agitated. But he was a coward. He didn't want to tell her the women she loved, those she considered her family, had lied to her for her entire life.

He leaned back into the cushions to let her look at his side. She peeled away the layer of leaves and tonics she'd applied, made a clicking noise with her tongue. "It's a bit red around the edges, but the bleeding has stopped. How fast do you usually heal?"

"I've never been stabbed before," he told her.

She grimaced. Pressed her fingertips to his skin. Evan felt his stomach tighten at her touch.

"It isn't hot," she said. "I don't think there's infection. Does it hurt?"

It didn't. Having her hands on him was not that sort of torment. "No. I'm sure it's fine."

He started to pull his shirt back into place, but Circe laid her hand over his to stop him. "I want to put some more ointment over it before you sleep. Just to be safe."

Evan nodded. He couldn't look at her. She was too close. She smelled of citrus and mint, and something that reminded him of warm cider. He didn't know which were from the mixing she'd done, and which belonged to her. Gods help him, he wanted to sniff her hair. He cleared his throat.

Circe looked at him. There was a strange tilt to the corner of her mouth, like she was concentrating very hard.

"Ready?" she asked.

"Knock yourself out."

Circe dabbed her fingertips into a container from her side table and spread it carefully over his wound. She wiped her hands on a clean white towel, and then, instead of leaves and woven fabric, placed a square of sterile gauze over it with tape. Her fingertips lingered, tracing the edges of the bandage, and then farther out. Her thumb pressed against his abdomen, too low, and Evan thought he had never been tested so much.

"Circe," he said.

She stilled, seemingly startled, and pulled her hands free. She wiped them again on the dish towel, shaking her head a little before standing to clean up the mess. Evan took a steadying breath and lowered the hem of his shirt.

She tossed the trash into the waste bin, reaching beside him for the discarded gauze packaging. The black mark on her hand caught his eye.

"What is that?"

She blushed but folded a knee to sit on the couch beside him. "That is my official Resident of Havenwood Falls tattoo. All the cool kids get them." She narrowed her eyes. "I'm pretty sure you're breaking the law right now not having one, actually."

She held her hand forward so Evan could examine the tiny flowing script.

He took her fingers in his. "Jump?"

Her cheeks colored further, but maybe not from embarrassment. "It's from a Bradbury quote. 'Go to the edge of the cliff and jump off. Build your wings on the way down.'"

"Books," he said. "She likes to curl up alone with a good book." He didn't let go of her hand.

She quirked a brow. "You think because a girl likes books it means she's not daring? She's not trouble?"

"Actually," he said, "I'm sure it's quite the opposite."

Her skin was flush, her eyes glittering in the dim light. Loose strands of hair had pulled free of their knot, tickling the line of her jaw. Evan's fingers touched her palm, his thumb lay against the delicate tattoo. It was her ring finger. *Jump*, it said.

Jump.

Circe's jaw shifted behind her lips. She was biting the inside of her cheek. Evan let his thumb run from the base of her ring finger down, back up again. He was going to tug her to him. He knew he shouldn't, but there it was. He was powerless to stop himself.

Circe swallowed hard, then was suddenly on her feet. She clutched the wad of gauze in her other hand. "Evan, I think—I think we should get some sleep."

He let go of her.

She seemed relieved.

It felt like ice water. "I'm sorry, Circe. Thank you . . . for everything."

She pressed her lips together, nodded. And then she clicked off the room's only remaining lamp to put herself in shadow. Evan pulled the throw from the back of the couch over him, but his eyes remained slits as he watched her place their mugs in the sink and close her bedroom door. The lock clicked shut.

Trouble, he thought. *So much trouble.*

CHAPTER 7

*C*irce lay awake in her queen-size bed, staring at the darkened ceiling. There was a man in the next room. A man she'd convinced herself was no good for her. A man she had touched. A man who had laid bare the darkness of his life, and, somehow, had still been able to share his childhood wishes and dreams with her.

Circe hadn't admitted aloud that she had dreamed about him more than once, and not in the weird, creepy stalker sort of way.

She remembered that rebellious phase she'd talked so casually about. She remembered the terms of the curse, its edict that forming a bond with a man—falling for him—would bring her doom. Its warning of the dark things that would come.

The last thing Circe needed was Evan Grey in the room next to her. The last thing she could do was make herself stop thinking about him.

It had been hours and hours since the awful incident that had brought them together, and Circe had nearly forgotten about it. All they had done was sit together and talk. He'd told her everything.

And what he hadn't told her then, he'd told her earlier—when he'd been under the influence of her potions.

Graceful, he'd said then. *Lovely.*

Circe had heard the words before. The witches who raised her had said it all the time. Morgan had told her she had eyes a man would drown in some day. Tia said that her smile could make the stars in the sky jealous. But they had a flair for the dramatic and only two speeds: everything was categorically the best or absolutely the worst. To hear the words from Evan was something else. To feel his touch was exactly *categorically the best* and *absolutely the worst* at once. Circe couldn't let this keep going. She had to stop. She had to make him leave.

She'd do it first thing in the morning.

Circe stared at the ceiling, the purpling light moving across in a thin strip. Morning was coming. Dawn was already here. Soon she'd have to face Evan again. She pressed her palms down on the blanket. She needed to just lie here and get some sleep. She would deal with it when she woke up. And then a terrible thought came to her: what if Evan woke before her? He'd be alone in her apartment. Had she left anything out? Anything potentially embarrassing or that he really shouldn't see? She'd barely had a chance to unpack, but she'd not brought much with her. She did a mental scan of the apartment and cringed when she thought of her sketchpad on the hall table. Gods, were there any drawings of him in it? She'd tried not to stare at him when he had followed her. She hadn't wanted to clue him in that she was on to him. The thing with being targeted, was that it was best to know where your attacker was coming from. She'd kept her eye on him the way he did her: covertly.

That didn't mean there weren't rough outlines of scruffy men in sunglasses and jackets with the collar drawn up all over those pages. Pages he could open to. Pages he could see. She cursed inwardly and flipped the comforter back.

She'd go get the sketchbook, and that was it. She wouldn't look at him. She wouldn't touch him. She'd only retrieve the incriminating evidence and then go to sleep.

She crept barefoot through the hallway, lights off despite the unfamiliar layout of her new apartment. She ran a hand over the bar that separated the kitchen from the living area and heard Chompers snoring in his bed across the room. She turned the corner to the short corridor between there and the doorway, and reached out blindly until she felt the edge of the hall table. She fumbled to right the small glass jar she knocked into, then touched the telltale metal spiral that bound her sketchbook. She sighed with relief.

Clutching it to her chest, she edged back toward the bedroom. At the end of the corridor, she looked in the darkness toward Evan's form.

In that moment, she couldn't help but think, What if the curse was right? What if Evan could cost her everything?

What if it wasn't?

What if this was all the life she'd ever live?

The lamp clicked on in the living room.

Circe caught her breath, thanking the gods she'd left on the black leggings instead of switching to her favorite bulldog-printed Christmas pajamas Louisa had gotten her as a joke.

"Don't you ever sleep?" Evan asked.

She nodded jerkily. "Just, uh, getting my notebook for some stuff I need to jot down."

Evan had been watching her for weeks. He surely knew the thing in her hand marked with "Sketch" in giant block letters was not a notebook.

"How's your side?"

"Fine," he said. "Doesn't really hurt at all now. You do great work."

She felt her bare toes drag across the hardwood, one foot curling behind the other. "It's nothing. Been doing those since I was a kid." She'd had harder spells, ones that had gone terribly wrong. Ointments were easy. No one lost a limb or turned an ugly hue if you mixed those a little too light or a little too strong.

"There's something I need to tell you," Evan admitted. "I should have said so before."

Suddenly, Circe was terrified whatever he said would be the end. He was too stiff, determined. He was going to leave. He was going to say he'd changed his mind about whose side he was on.

Circe felt it like a knife in her chest. She'd just decided it was time to end this, hadn't she? So why, now, could she not recall the reasons? Words tumbled from her of their own accord. "What about you?"

His brow drew together. "What?"

"Sleeping," she said. "Don't you ever sleep?" Her quiet laugh echoed through the room. "I mean, following me around every day couldn't have left you much time. Do you not need sleep? Is it your . . . the . . ." She found herself waving a hand toward him to encompass his *condition*. She couldn't seem to say the word *curse*.

Evan stared at her.

She waited.

"Yeah," he said. "I guess I don't need as much. Circe, I—"

"What about food?" she said. "Do you need less food? Or more?"

Evan crossed the room, coming to rest an arm's length in front of her.

"I wonder how else it affects you. Do you know the words she used? Or maybe the ingredients—" She stopped short, realizing her nervous jabbering had gone too far. It was probably rude to ask the victim of a hex about his perpetrator.

Evan put a hand over hers to still the twitching. Over her

sketchbook, its pages scattered with drawings of him. She swallowed hard.

When had she started watching him so closely? When had she decided he was something deserving of those attentions? Her gaze met his, and Circe knew she'd been lying to herself for weeks. She'd been interested in his presence since she'd first caught sight of him.

Evan seemed to notice he was reaching across the distance to touch her and dropped his hand.

"Circe," he said, his voice like a caress over her skin. She didn't want to hear what was coming.

She knew she had to.

She inched closer, entirely too aware of the space he was taking up in the room. His presence was a bonfire, and Circe's soul yearned for nothing more than heat. "What is it?"

She had a few thoughts of what she wanted his words to be. *I need to tell you how much I yearn to touch you, to taste your lips, to trace the lines of your face.* And she had a few thoughts of what she should do in response. Somewhere in the back of her mind, she understood the wisest would have been to lock herself in her room and call someone who'd slap some sense into her. She was pretty sure Morgan would happily do it.

At the thought, a loud *whack* echoed through the room. Circe's heart skipped, and Evan's posture went suddenly protective. They looked together toward the corridor, at the oak-handled broom that now lay across the wood-plank floor.

A portent.

Evan was beside her now, the warmth of his palm against her back. She looked at him, so close it was painful, and whispered, "Company's coming."

"Circe," he said again.

It was all he got out before the door to the apartment slammed open.

"Circe!" the witches shouted in a scattered harmony.

Morgan was through the door first, her raven hair slick against a thick wool cloak. "Darling, it's freezing here. You should really come home."

Tia pushed past her, elbowing briskly on the way. "Pshh. Do not listen to her. This weather is wonderful. But your wards are the absolute worst."

They swarmed the living room, six of them, and Louisa jerked her away from Evan to crush her in a hug.

"Oh, you look amazing," Anise cooed. "I just want to squeeze your little cheeks."

"Wait your turn," Louisa hissed.

Circe was being jostled, and shuffled, and moved farther from Evan with every single step.

"What are you all doing here?" she managed beneath the aunts' grip.

"Well, we're here to help you, of course," Morgan snapped.

Tia leaned in, craning her neck to see around Anise. "We heard you got attacked by a shifter. Did you use a hemlock for your elixir base? Nightshade?"

"I didn't poison him."

"What?" four of the witches said in unison. Tia pouted. "Why not?"

"He was incapacitated. I just put a minor illusion on him, and Evan threw him out the window until the Court could take care of it."

Six pair of eyes moved to the only man in the room. The *Evan*.

"Did someone from the Court call you?" Circe asked the aunts. "How did you even get here? How is everyone coming though the town wards?"

Anise patted Circe's hand. "You look lovely, dear. So happy to see you. We've missed you dreadfully. Why, Hazel has practically withered away."

"It's only been a few days."

She ran a hand over Circe's dark hair. "Time is strange that way, isn't it?"

Circe heard whispers over their conversation, three of the aunts hissing about shifters and windows, while Morgan said something to Evan. She had him by the corridor, walking toward him in a bid to remove him from the room.

"I know what you're hiding," Evan said in a harsh tone.

Morgan's reply was hushed, but Circe heard it anyway. "You know *nothing*."

Circe pushed past Anise, trying to see beyond Tia's mop of fuzzy red curls.

"You have to tell her," Evan hissed.

Morgan smiled, and it was terrifying. "Say good day, Mr. Grey. It's time to go."

He was up against the door now, and his eyes met Circe's through the gathered chaos of a half dozen witches. Circe nodded. She didn't want Evan to go. But he couldn't be here. Not with them. Not when they found out who he was tied to. Circe didn't know how much the aunts already knew, but Morgan's use of his full name was not an accident. The aunts had their ways.

And just because they weren't a danger to her didn't mean they weren't dangerous.

Evan needed to go.

He frowned, but he did not argue. She wanted to call to him, to say . . . something. She just didn't know what. But he was gone, the door sealed behind him, and the aunts corralled her once again.

"You didn't have to bring everyone," she said.

"Oh." Tia waved a hand. "I know you're doing that sarcasm thing you're so fond of, but we actually did bring everyone. The others are down in their cars. *Someone*—and I won't say who, dear, even if you twist my arm—came into the parking area a little too hot and caught the side of a couple of light posts."

Circe cringed. "Are they hurt?"

"No, not at all. They're made of concrete, dear. I tell you, whoever built this complex did a wonderful job."

Circe blinked. She looked to Louisa, who only smiled.

In a matter of moments—at the drop of a broom—Circe's old world and new had collided spectacularly. She wanted to cry, but she wasn't certain if it was from happiness or despair. The echo of a car horn rose to her window from the lot below, and Circe could hear the catcalls being thrown at the man who'd just left her apartment. She slapped her palm to her face to cover the grimace.

"Seriously," she said to the room. "You all are not fit for public."

Tia swirled around her as Anise opened the pantry to examine each and every mug.

"Too bad," Tia sing-songed, "because we're going to a fes-ti-val."

"What?" Circe crossed her arms. "You can't be serious. I thought you said you were here to help me."

"Yes, dear. Of course we are," Anise said from the kitchen.

Louisa took Circe's hand. She felt a little like she was being passed around the room. It was dizzying to be in the presence of so many of the aunts at once.

It always had been.

Louisa said, "We weren't planning, of course, but on the way into town we saw the sign, and well, we took it as a sign, sign that it was. It will work perfectly."

Circe started to ask, "Perfectly for what?" but couldn't get a word in before Morgan took the conversation up. "The Into the Mystic New Age and Psychic Fair. Perfect indeed."

Louisa tugged Circe's hand to get her attention. "It is the spring equinox, dear. Did you forget?"

Circe had forgotten. She'd lost track of everything. All she could think of was Evan and this new life.

Every year on the equinox, the aunts had done a special ritual to bolster the protections they'd laid on Circe since she was a child. She assumed that would be over now, that she'd be responsible for setting those protections herself, since she was living on her own.

She sighed. So far she'd been doing a bang-up job.

Tia sprung up beside her, lavender mug of hot tea in hand. "You look ragged around the eyes, dear. Haven't been getting enough sleep?"

Had she not been so distracted, Circe would have noticed the hint of valerian and poppy in the air. But she took a sip out of habit, and by the time she realized, she was being dragged limply into her bed.

"No worries, sweetest. Have a nap and then we'll go to the fair."

She muttered something horrid in reply, but the women surrounding her bed only giggled.

"She's getting to be a grown-up, that one. My, my, how time does spend."

The click of a light switch sounded across the room, and the darkness behind Circe's eyelids intensified.

Damn it, she thought. *Drugged.*

CHAPTER 8

$\mathcal{E}$van left the apartment, fuming and dealing with a building determination he knew was going to get him into even more trouble than he was already in. He'd promised himself he wouldn't do this again, but here he was, risking his own neck by sticking his fool self in the middle of someone else's business. He should have just told Circe who was after her and left.

He should have never stayed.

And now it was too late. He was involved. There was no stopping it.

He was going to help her.

It was early, the air cool and the rising sun throwing long shadows over the sidewalk when he walked past the Haven Saloon. It was probably a good thing it wasn't open yet with the mood he was in, but he would come back later to get some food. Right now, he needed a shower and a place to think. A large Victorian manor sat diagonally off the square, the sign proclaiming it Whisper Falls Inn. It was too far from Circe's apartment for Evan's liking, but he knew there was nothing to be done for her with a dozen witches at her ear. He'd parked his truck on a nearby side street when he first arrived, moving it occasionally so as not to draw attention. He stopped there first to get his backpack with a change of clothes.

He was given a second-floor room at the inn and a speculative look from the gray-eyed brunette who checked him in. He couldn't focus on why, though, because on the counter was a flyer for a local festival. A festival that celebrated the spring equinox.

An equinox when a mage might perform a ritual to increase its potency.

A deadline.

The deadline was today.

Evan cursed, dropped the key to his room in his pocket, and turned to go back outside. He had tried to speak with the witches and was ushered straight out of Circe's life. But there was someone else Circe trusted, and they knew enough about the supernatural world to remove a spelled coyote from outside her building without investigations, or the law. Evan would find this Court of the Sun and the Moon and warn them, even if the witches who raised Circe wouldn't.

He stepped again into the morning sun and realized the town square was already bustling with people starting their days, opening businesses, and preparing for the festival. He decided to cut around the foot traffic by going behind the shops. He crossed Main Street, following it east, and kept close to the building until he found the alley. His pace was brisk, and he'd formed a full resolve.

Nothing was going to stop Evan Grey from preventing the evil Circe's father was trying to bring onto them all.

Something struck his leg, like the sting of a wasp, and he smacked at it in instinct. His hand brushed the tip of a small dart, its fletch turkey feather tucked into lightweight metal. He yanked it free of his skin, eyes snapping up to find the dart's source. Heat spread up Evan's thigh, crossing his skin like fire. A shadow rushed toward him, and he dropped his backpack to shift. The cold of the hex shot through him, icy fingers that traced his bones.

It was always a shock, the pain when the hex pulled and snapped his skeleton, distorted his size and shaped his body into something other than what he was. It knocked him off balance, and he widened his stance, throwing his hands to the side as they broke into fur and claws, as his arms became too long for a man. Evan's neck wrenched, lifting his face to the sky as his jaw remade itself with fangs, then forward again as his neck took on the rigid spikes. His back widened, spreading his shoulders and ripping his shirt.

And then the frigid hex slammed into the heat of the poison in his leg.

Evan fell, grabbing his thigh as the hex and the toxin collided. His leg was flesh, his fingers fur, and his body felt like it was being crushed by the weight of that battle. A massive being slammed into him, and Evan knew right away it was a demon. The thing sank claws into his gut to drag Evan against the back of a building. He was trapped, unable to shift because of the poison and unable to stay partially transformed because the pain of it was stealing every bit of energy from him. He had no choice but to let the shift retreat, but before he did, he took one good swipe at the being's gnarled face.

Its skin was the color of rot, and its eyes were black. It wore a trench coat and jeans, but if the being thought it was fooling anyone, it was dead wrong. It pushed Evan up the wall, sliding his shifting form with long horrible claws.

"You're making a mistake," Evan told the thing when his mouth was once more that of a man. His voice was raspy, owing to the shift, the poison, and those cursed talons spearing his gut. "She's just a witch."

The thing smiled at him. "She has the blood of the gods. I can smell it on her."

"Lucius is no god," Evan spat.

The thing laughed. "Which is why he needs the girl."

Evan pressed his boots into the wall behind him, launching himself forward to slam into the demon. They rolled across the alleyway, and the demon's claws tore free of Evan's gut. Blood soaked what was left of his shirtfront; he knew without the shift he wouldn't be able to properly heal the wound until he slept.

"Stay away from her," Evan warned.

"It is too late for that. The ceremony is near. The council waits."

The demon shoved a blast of power into Evan's chest, melting the patch of asphalt beneath him. At that close range, it was all he could do to withstand it. Flashes of his first shift, of the blood and claws and pain, and of every shift after crashed through Evan's mind. He could not allow himself to die; the moment this creature was done with him, it would be headed for Circe.

And if this beast was right, if Circe's line was that of a god, Lucius would bleed her out to feed the runes etched across his skin. Evan had spent enough time with the witch who'd hexed him to know that.

Evan curled in on himself, and the demon moved to make the final blow. Evan grabbed the vial from his boot and smashed it on the concrete. Lucius had given it to him—gods knew why. And now it crawled up the demon's leg like acid, burning through its flesh. Evan reached for his other boot, drawing out a thin blade, also a spelled gift from Circe's father. To protect Evan from her. From the dangerous, deadly witch.

Evan thrust the blade into the demon's chest and watched it turn to dust and ash.

He rolled onto his back, panting, and closed his eyes to the morning sun. Lucius was not a god. That meant Circe's mother must have had some trace of god's blood in her line. If she was of a goddess's bloodline, even heavily diluted, it would be potent enough to perform a dangerous rite. It would give Lucius the power he'd been craving. Too much power. Enough to destroy more than just a girl or a curse.

Lucius Hallewell was going to bleed out Circe for a ritual.

His own daughter.

Evan rolled to his side, retched onto the ground, then dragged himself to his pack. He couldn't pass out here. He needed sleep to heal, and he needed to cover this blood before someone discovered him.

He needed to find Circe.

CHAPTER 9

*C*irce woke refreshed and clearheaded, with a desire to wring those dirty witches' necks. It didn't happen, though, because the moment she opened her bedroom door, she was accosted with the overwhelming presence of thirteen women. Her tiny apartment living room was practically crawling with them. The aunts were draped over her sofa, her chair, making a circle of haphazard poses around her tiny coffee table, now littered with candles and cards. Chompers was panting happily on his bed, with what looked like a week's worth of steak in his bowl. Circe sighed, getting her first taste of the orange and lilac haze that filled the kitchen, then noticed all of the apartment's smoke detectors lay disassembled on the bar that divided the space.

"You could have just taken the batteries out," Circe said to the room.

The aunts shouted out greetings to her, and the room seemed to spin as they took to their feet, cloaks and tunics and scarves swirling as they dressed for the weather outdoors. "Get ready," they said. "We've been waiting *an eternity.*"

Circe glared at them.

"How did you even get here? I thought the wards made this town nearly impossible for outsiders to locate."

Tia nodded. "They really do, dear. Those wards are perfectly stout. I can feel this town buzzing through my veins." Her hands came up to demonstrate, as if Circe could see the sense of magic Tia was feeling. She explained, "But Lyra invited us here and told us how to find our way. We couldn't miss the equinox."

Anise cleared her throat. "We may not be able to remember the town after time and the castings drag it into haze, so Lyra agreed to remind us." She smiled sweetly. "And we could never forget you, love."

Circe crossed her arms. "So the Beaumonts can know you're coming for a visit, but not me."

Morgan smirked, flipping a tarot card.

Hazel peeked around the corner to the corridor, giving Circe an unrepentant grin. "You must have slept for hours, dear. Hurry and dress, we want to get to the festival before the equinox."

Circe looked at the clock. "It's barely noon."

Hazel nodded emphatically. "Exactly. Now go!"

Circe pressed her fingers to the bridge of her nose, and then turned back toward her bedroom. A trail of leaves and jasmine crossed the threshold of her room.

"I can lay my own wards," she said over her shoulder.

"Let Louisa have her fun," someone called from the crowded kitchen. "She never gets to do anything for you anymore."

Circe closed the door behind her and went to the bathroom to splash cold water on her face. She was an adult. She could handle this. She would not let the aunts take over her new life. She should have already protected herself against sleeping concoctions.

She should have never taken that tea.

She reached into the vanity drawer, took out a bracelet, and wrapped it three times around her wrist. She hung the malachite pendant around her neck. The aunts had shown her their methods her entire life. They could only best her if she was willing to let them. She ran a brush through her tangled hair and put balm on her lips. She would enjoy them for their company, and as soon as this festival was over, she would send them on their way. She would have a talk with Addie about giving her a heads up when the aunts were making a plan.

Circe bit her lip, glancing in the mirror. Thoughts of Evan drifted up, but she pressed them back down. Whatever that was would have to wait.

The moment she exited the bedroom, wearing jeans and a thick-knit sweater, the witches ushered her out of the apartment and down the stairs. Louisa slipped a narrow bottle of dust into Circe's front jeans pocket, whispering, "just in case," as the others argued about how best to arrive. It was only a few blocks to the park, and with more than a dozen in their party, they decided not to drive. Though Circe knew from experience, when the aunts hit a festival, it was good to have a cargo van nearby.

"Who's going to buy the most today?" she asked.

"Hazel!" Three voices shouted in unison, while several more denied that they would spend one single cent. She could hear the music already, and as they walked toward the square, the sound of "Touch of Grey" grew. They found its source in a local food truck: Tacos for Daze. It was brightly painted and parked in front of the Haven Saloon, and Circe walked right up and asked for two tacos. There were groans of complaints from her party. "Are you seriously going to stop at the very first vendor?" And, "Tacos? Where's your sense of adventure?"

Circe smiled. "Tacos are their own adventure, Anise."

Then three of the witches ordered Sugar Magnolia Margaritas.

"So," Morgan said, "I see it's going to be one of *those* kind of days."

Tia twirled around her tauntingly, the margarita glass spinning along levelly and not spilling a drop. "The absolute best. I assure you."

They traipsed through melting patches of snow toward Town Square Park, and even Circe began to feel the excitement of the festival. They had been her favorite times as a child, one of the rare opportunities she'd had to run freely and act like a kid. The aunts had a terrible habit of getting distracted, and they'd always stuck Hazel with the job of keeping an eye on her. It was not the woman's best skill.

The park was crowded with booths, each so colorful and enticing, the aunts could not agree on where to start.

"It's not yet one o'clock," Louisa said. "We have plenty of time to look around and still get back together before the big event."

Morgan gave her a fierce side-eye, but the group split into three smaller ones anyway, after much banter that unfamiliar onlookers might assume was near violent warfare.

Circe left them to it, walking with Anise down a table filled with crystals and candles. There were covered tents farther down, and booths displaying herbs and teas, books and jewelry.

A brunette dressed in jade, bejeweled and scarved, flashed them a smile. "Want to know your future?"

Tia jumped and squealed, her palms slapping together. "Oh, yes! Me, please."

The woman's gaze ran over the group, and Tia began the questioning. Who was she, what could she do, why had she chosen purple for the tent, how many moons crossed its surface.

"I'm Callie," she answered with a laugh. "And how about we start with a reading and go from there?"

Tia grabbed Anise's arm, but Anise shook her head. "You go ahead. I can tell you'll be in good hands with Callie."

Circe bit down a grin. Anise had never trusted other fortune tellers. If she wanted to know something, she read it in the leaves so she could do her own interpretations of the signs.

They kept walking, breathing it all in. Circe let the spring sun and the sound of the crowd fill her with that unmistakable festival atmosphere. Banners proclaimed *Past Life Readings*, *Find Your Spirit Guide*, and *Healing Massage*. Circe saw Addie among the crowd, casual in her jeans and a hoodie, its graphic a waxing crescent moon. Circe gave her a wave, but was tugged along by the witches as they followed the sound of "Brown Eyed Girl" farther into the festivities.

She couldn't keep herself from swaying to the rhythm and humming along. She passed a few more familiar faces, startled to realize Havenwood Falls was already beginning to feel comfortable. Despite what had happened, despite the turmoil of the last twenty-four hours, it felt like *home*.

It was a good feeling.

Circe smiled and let herself sing about slipping and sliding along a waterfall. Her voice was echoed by a petite woman with graying auburn hair. She wore bright leggings under a long top, and though she looked less like a fortune teller than some of the others, she stood in front of a colorful tent proclaiming her Eloise Sinclair of Into the Mystic New Age Books and Gifts, the festival's namesake. The crowd steered Circe away from a psychic reading, and she was distracted once again by the sights and sounds.

A small girl was handing out honeyed candies for an herbal shop vendor, and Circe popped one into her mouth. She'd lost track of Anise, but she was sure they were all close by. She wasn't a little girl anymore, and you couldn't truly lose a pack of witches that big in a town this small.

Her eyes were drawn to a tall oaken cabinet, its top windowed on three sides to reveal a mannequin decked out with scarves and glittering beads. Circe grinned at the absurdity, knowing full well there were actual clairvoyants—women like Callie and Eloise—right here in Havenwood Falls. She came closer. The mannequin was draped in purple, her lips too red, her eyeshadow too blue. Her face was turned down, her plastic hands spangled with rings two to a finger where they hovered over a glowing crystal ball. Her nails were lacquered that same purple as the ball, and Circe found herself mesmerized by the color, the light of it.

She was standing in front of the machine now, a strange yearning in her heart that she did not understand. The mannequin's hands moved, its arms shifting in that jerky, mechanical way, the music-box melody clashing with the Van Morrison coming out of the festival's speakers. Color swirled inside the globe of the crystal ball, there was a strange *click*, and the mannequin's hands lurched to a sudden stop.

A ticket came out of the machine. Circe glanced around, but no one was paying her any mind. She leaned forward, tugging the card from the delivery slot. It had come out upside down, displaying the familiar tarot image of the Tower. Circe flipped the card over and read the message on her fortune.

The curse does not lie within you. It was borne of the coven.

Circe stared at the message, feeling like her bones had turned to ash.

The curse does not lie within you.

It was borne of the coven.

Her coven.

CHAPTER 10

*E*van woke in a darkened room, his face plastered to the tile floor. The smell of cleaning supplies and bleached cotton towels clued him in, brought back the memory of checking in. The gray-eyed attendant. The Victorian manor.

Whisper Falls Inn.

He wasn't sure how he'd made it back there, but he was glad he had. He rolled over, staring at the ceiling in the spare light that came through the bathroom door. His backpack was on the floor beside him, contents strewn across the tile. He was pretty sure he'd forgotten to get his phone out of his ruined jacket in the alley, though he couldn't think of anyone he would actually call. He needed to find Circe. He stumbled to his feet, finding the clock on the nightstand beside the ornate headboard. It was nearly one o'clock. He was dangerously short on time.

He flicked on the light switch and saw the mess of his clothes, the dried blood covering his healing flesh. He knew he'd never make it across the square like that, so he peeled off the ragged material to shower off the blood.

He wasted precious time checking her apartment, and then

following the trail of witches who had taken her to the festival in the park. When he finally found her, she was surrounded by them, and Evan had to hide behind the tents and banners until she moved out on her own. She'd been arm-in-arm with the blonde he'd thought was named Anise, Hazel close on their heels. Morgan was speaking with some locals three booths down—the tattoo artist and two silver-haired women wearing business attire. He'd watched Circe meander through the crowds, laughing and singing as if she wasn't in imminent danger from her murderous father.

Then Circe had walked away from the others, seemingly in a trance as she headed for an old-fashioned fortune machine the likes of which Evan had only seen in movies. "Madame Mystic" was painted in purple script on the thin metal signs nailed above the box's windows. Circe was smiling, and then she wasn't. She leaned forward, drew a card from the ticket slot.

Evan watched in horror as Circe turned to ash.

He stepped forward, torn between fear and action, but he realized what appeared to be ash was only a cloud of smoke—the way he'd seen Circe hide the small bird so many weeks ago. Evan could feel something horrible crawl over his skin. It was a premonition, or maybe the feeling of it from Circe, but she was scared or hurt or something else that was very, very wrong. He rushed to her—to the hazy fog that was Circe—and tried to take her in his arms. He whispered her name, but if the witches noticed they did not look his way. Circe came into form, at least he thought she had—but it was he who turned to ash. His hands where they touched her were gray now, the same smoke that disguised her figure. She was hiding him. Hiding them both. *From what?*

"Evan," she whispered, and the pain in her voice was more than he could bear. He pulled her against him and turned to walk away from whatever it was that had upset her so badly. They stepped over a pile of cards like the one she'd held in her hands only a moment before, but Evan only saw the same image on all: two naked forms, a tree behind each form.

Circe was crying.

Evan took her to the inn, her cloaking spell allowing them to get to his room unnoticed. The space was small, holding only a queen-size bed, a wooden dresser, a narrow desk, and a chair. They sat on the edge of the bed, and Evan slid his arm around her. The smoke covering them dissipated.

He let her sit there, let her think through whatever it was she was concentrating on so hard, and kept his hand against her so that she knew he was there should she need him. It was painful to see her hurting, and the idea that he had gotten so attached to her was terrifying. Everything about her scared the hell out of Evan in the most satisfying way. Like her tattoo. Like jumping from a cliff and hoping for wings on the way down. Being near Circe had opened something inside Evan without his realization, and now, it was as if he could finally breathe free.

She hadn't been crying hard, but eventually she wiped her cheek with the back of her hand to look up at him. Her lashes were damp, the tip of her nose just a little pink.

"They lied to me, Evan."

Her hands were folded tightly in her lap; he reached to take one in his. "I'm sorry. I should have told you."

"My whole life." She let out a harsh breath. "I'm so mad at them. And there's nothing I can do. It's over, already done. Anything I did now would just be revenge."

Evan slid his hand slowly up her back, down again. He did not know what to say. She was right. She knew she was.

"I don't want to be that person. I don't ever want anyone to make me that person. I just—I just want them to have not done this to me."

She was breathing more easily now, the shock of it gone, only the hurt and disappointment left. She leaned into Evan's side.

Her fingers twisted to twine with his where they lay in her lap. She traced a thumb over his knuckles one by one methodically in between her slow breaths.

An onyx charm lay against her wrist, the rest of the bracelet hidden beneath her sleeve.

After a moment, she smiled up at him with chagrin. "I'm sorry," she said. "I just broke into your room and cried all over your stuff." She ran her fingers over her hair. "I must look a mess."

Evan pulled her hand down. "You look lovely."

She blushed. "Do you mind if I . . ." She gestured toward the restroom, and Evan drew his embrace free to let her go.

He heard her splashing water, then silence as he imagined she was drying her face. Then there was a lighter sound, and between the aged insulation in the inn's walls and his sensitive hearing, Evan realized she was whispering. He tried not to listen, he really did. But words snuck through, broken only by the thunder of his heart.

"It's okay . . . don't let them take this from you . . . let yourself be with him . . . take your life back . . . live for you . . . let yourself *feel* for once . . ."

He searched frantically for the television remote—anything to create noise. He wanted badly to clear his throat so that she'd understand how thin the walls were, but he couldn't seem to get enough air. What was she doing? Giving herself a pep talk? Gods, why had he brought her into his hotel room? This wasn't what he'd meant to do. He was hexed; she was a witch. This was a terrible, terrible idea. He caught sight of himself in the mirror over the dresser, all damp hair and flushed skin. The latch to the bathroom door clicked, and Evan jumped, turning to face her, television remote finally in hand. She saw his expression.

"It's okay," she told him. "I'm angry at them, but this isn't revenge. I feel safe with you, Evan. We don't have to worry about the curse."

He felt himself deflate. She'd been worried about his hex. Had she thought he might shift on her? Had she thought he might actually hurt her? Turn into a beast and tear through her tender flesh? The idea of it made him ill.

"Circe," he started, then had to stop. He swallowed hard. "I would never hurt you. I know why I came here, what I am, and why I followed you, but I swear to you, even as a beast, I would never—could not hurt you."

She gave a surprised half laugh. "Oh, Evan, I never thought for a moment you could. Not in that way."

He opened his mouth to say, "What?" but she was moving toward him, and all thought ceased.

The remote fell to the floor.

Circe crossed the space between them, her face bright and open, her eyes only for him. She stopped barely a few inches from him, waited. He let his hand raise to her cheek, let his fingers sink into her chestnut hair. She smelled of spring and of the festival, of the oils and fragrances that had been on display. Her sweater was soft and black and only made her skin more luminous, her cheeks more pink. She looked up at him, no rush or anger in her gaze. True to her word, she had placed her hurt out of mind. She was letting herself be free.

He was more grateful for this moment than he had ever been for any of his life. He wanted to confess to her, to tell her all the things he had done, but she already knew. She knew about the hex, she knew what was in his blood. She had accepted him despite those things.

There would be no debts here. She was not offering herself in exchange for anything; she was giving them both the gift of freedom, for however long that might be.

The pad of his thumb crossed her lips, trailing down as he let his fingertips trace her flesh. She watched him, and it dragged out the moment, letting it feel like an eternity of exploration. He leaned down, tasting her. Her mouth parted beneath his, and it was sweetened honey. She was warm and soft, and she rose into his kiss just the slightest bit. Like the patience she'd given him was ebbing, like her warmth was pressing slowly to heat.

Her hands rose to his sides, sliding beneath the hem of his shirt to find his skin. Evan sucked in a breath at her touch and realized he too was becoming unduly eager. He wanted to touch every part of her, wanted to feel her bare skin. Gods, he wanted to see her naked and sprawled across his bed. Their kiss deepened, and she was pressed against him, and still it wasn't enough.

Evan's hands slid up her back beneath that sweater, pulled her closer. She stood on tiptoe, climbing on top of his boots. They were both breathing too fast, their pulses pounding in a rhythm he should not have been able to feel.

Circe drew back from their kiss, sighing deeply. She bit her lip, watching him through her lashes as she toed off the heel of one boot. The bit lip turned to a wicked smile as she kicked off the other. Evan clumsily followed suit as she pulled him toward the bed.

She fell before him on a flat white comforter, her hair spilling over it, her arms stretching beside her to brush the fabric.

"I've never slept in a hotel," she confessed.

Evan's smirk answered she would not be getting that sleep right now.

She threw her head back and laughed, full and genuine. It exposed her neck and the line of her jaw. Evan climbed onto the bed beside her, carefully sliding his hand up her thigh and over her hip. He squeezed and drew her to face him, so they were side by side on the bed. A green pendant on a chain around her neck slid sideways; Circe saw him looking.

"I took precautions," she said, "after my apartment was busted into."

"Do you think they'll be able to find you here?"

She shrugged one shoulder, let her hand climb to his waist. "Not if I've done my castings well."

It made him feel a little better. He would be at her side, and he'd left his cell phone—the only means to track him—in the alley behind those shops.

"And what if they do?" he asked.

She smiled. "Let them come. I am not afraid of them."

He leaned forward to brush his lips over hers. "And what of me? What if I never let you go?"

A shiver ran through him, and he had the oddest sensation it was not his own. Circe breathed her reply against his lips. "What if you don't?"

What if you don't?

Evan thought in that moment there was nothing more likely in the world.

He took her mouth with his, pressing her to her back as he held himself over her, and Circe arched into him, curling her knees around his waist as quick as a cat. He broke their kiss to grin at her, and she drew her sweater over her head, throwing it off the edge of the bed. Evan felt the crush in his chest when he saw her there, hair loose over the white linens, skin as soft and sweet as he'd imagined. He drew back further, running his hands over the sides of her lace-trimmed bra, down the curve of her waist, across the plane above her pants. Her stomach trembled, and when his fingers reached the fastener of her jeans, he looked up at her.

Her expression said it was agony, but only the best kind. He slid back and leaned over to kiss her above that waistband. Her breath hitched before being released in a sigh. He undid the button and zipper, and she lifted her hips for him. He kissed her again, trailing his mouth over her flesh as he pulled the jeans free. He repeated the process as he moved once more up her form, lingering longer this time at the delicate skin of her hips, her thighs, her stomach. Her panties were soft black satin, and Evan ran his kiss over those as well. Circe groaned, rose into him, and he kicked off his own jeans. He raised up to pull his shirt off, but he was only halfway out of it before Circe tugged him down. She yanked it over his head and took his mouth with hers.

"Evan," she whispered, and the sound of it said so much more. She couldn't wait any longer, and gods help him, even if he'd wanted to tease her, he couldn't wait either. They shuffled bedding and pillows, colliding as they went, unable to draw away from each other long enough to properly remove their clothes. But then they were bare, by sheer determination, and Evan had an instant of wild disbelief as he held himself over her, seeing her expression clouded by lust, her body entirely open to him. He let the naked desire show on his face as he touched her, running a hand over the slickness at the junction of her thighs. He had to close his eyes for a moment, to catch his breath at the unbearable heat, at how much she wanted him.

He leaned down once more to kiss her deeply, felt the press of her against him. He kept his hands on her hips as he straightened and slid, excruciatingly slowly, into her. She was so wet, so soft. Her arms slipped above her to the headboard, her body bowing upward as Evan thrust into her with building speed.

"Circe," he murmured, unable to form any other word. She pressed harder into him in reply, breathing out a throaty moan. It did not take long until they were both breathless, until their pleasure hit that plateau and was released with a low animal groan, and then Evan was beside her, holding her to him, kissing her face and touching her skin and never, never wanting to let her go.

Circe was naked except for the tangle of sheets and the jewels wrapped at her wrist and neck. She held her hand over her chest, as if she couldn't quite catch her breath. Evan's breathing became more regular, and he sensed something else, some strange scent in the air, metallic and sharp. He leaned up to look at Circe, her expression stricken.

"What is it?"

She stared at him, closed her eyes, and shook her head. "Oh, Evan. I've done it. I'm so sorry." Her eyes came open again, bright but crumpled at the edges in her distress. "I thought I was safe. I thought—I thought it would be okay."

He rose further, glanced around the room. "What are you talking about? Circe, what is it?"

She looked as if she was on the verge of tears.

"The curse," she said.

Evan jerked to sitting, turned his arms and hands. He was not shifting; no part of him felt the icy hex crawling through his blood. "You are safe. It's okay. You don't have to worry about the hex. I won't turn, not with you this close."

Her brow drew down. "What are you talking about?" And then she saw his stomach, with the pink healing lines and marks from that demon's claws. "What happened to you?" She spoke the words with surprise, raising up to sitting, same as him. She reached automatically toward his wounds, and her hand came free of her chest.

The pendant had exploded. She'd held her hand there to cover it.

"What was that?" Evan asked. "Circe, was that malachite?"

She met his gaze, expression unknowable, and nodded. "Bad

things are coming. I thought I was safe. I thought I could do this one thing." She swallowed hard. "I triggered the curse."

"Stop staying that. I told you I'm not shifting."

"Would you quit talking about shifting for one second? This is serious, Evan. What happened to your stomach?"

He ran a hand through his hair. "I was attacked, earlier this afternoon. The council sent a demon after me." *After you.*

Her eyes went wide.

"It's all right," he told her. "I took care of him. But there will be more." He laid his hand over hers. "You set protections, right? You're safe. You said they couldn't find you." He looked at the clock. "And once the equinox has passed, you should be safe for a while until we can figure out how to deal with this."

"The aunts," she said in a small voice. "Evan, I said the aunts couldn't find me." She clutched the sheet to her chest. "They lied to me, told me someone else had set my curse. It was them all along. I thought, I thought you said you knew . . ."

He stared at her, his heart cold. "I knew they were keeping a secret from you. A secret about the council and why they wanted your blood." Her words were seeping slowly through the confusion, falling into place in all the wrong order. "What you do you mean *your* curse?"

"You didn't know. About my curse." She was moving from the bed, gathering her clothes.

Evan wanted to stop her, but he found himself doing the same thing. There was a danger building in the air, and it wasn't just this revelation.

She looked up at him as she slid on her jeans. "You thought I meant your . . . thing." She gestured toward him, as if to encompass the hex that caused him to turn into a horrid beast with one mild flick of her wrist. As if this other curse was so much larger that the two could not even compare. "And I thought you meant—What is it? What did you think I already knew?"

Evan straightened, pulling his shirt down to cover the damage to his skin. "The council is coming for you. Today, for a ritual that must be done at the equinox."

She looked at the clock, back to him.

"Circe," he said. "There's something more."

The man who wants to kill you is your father.

She waited, eyes bright, for Evan to destroy her world.

There was a sudden vibration beneath them, the room's floor shifting as if from an earthquake. Circe turned from Evan, and both of them ran for the single door.

CHAPTER 11

*C*irce and Evan reached the end of the corridor before they realized the quaking had stopped. Or rather, they realized the rest of the hotel had never moved.

"They're trying to force us," Evan said. "He wants you on the run."

She glanced at the stairwell, wishing they weren't on the second floor. "They can't do it here. The inn is full of supernaturals. They'll want us outside." The idea of the equinox, of a blood rite on the same day the aunts had always protected her, niggled at the back of her mind. What would this council want to do that was tied to the same day? Circe's gaze, suddenly sharp, cut to Evan. "What do you mean *he*? I thought this was a whole council of mages."

Evan placed a hand on her elbow. His voice was full of regret. "Lucius," he said. "The council is headed by Lucius Hallewell."

Circe felt a strange chill run through her, settling in the pit of her gut. It made her a little queasy. "What?"

"I'm sorry. That was what I'd meant to tell you. The secret I thought the witches were keeping from you."

Circe remembered speaking the words, words she'd not told anyone else in the world but Evan.

Because she'd known better than to discuss her findings with the aunts. Knew any talk of her father would only hurt or annoy them, and cause a flurry of new restrictions on her free time and ability to do such research. They had kept it from her on purpose.

Her father.

She felt numb, the words falling from her mouth as she stared blankly down the empty corridor. "My father wants to use me in a ritual." She rolled the idea around for a moment, let it fall into place with everything she'd learned. Everything that was fact and everything the aunts had told her. Their utter disgust for even the idea of him. Evan waited, but Circe knew they needed to go. She had to make a decision. "Why would he leave me?" she asked. "If he wanted me, if he had some use for me and was going to try so hard to recover me—why not just keep me?"

She knew in her heart the answer, but she had to say it aloud. She needed Evan's confirmation of her fears.

"Your powers would not have manifested until this year." Evan's reply was careful. Circe heard what he did not say anyway. Circe knew the truth in her broken heart.

"They stole me. They knew what he'd been planning, and they took me when I was a child." That fit so much easier in her memory, fell into each tiny crack left by the things her aunts had never said. They'd done their ritual when they knew he'd need to do his. Had they been in league all along? Had they known Circe's mother? Had they loved her as one of their own?

Had she once been their thirteenth?

A rumble started at the opposite end of the hallway, crawling slowly toward them. Circe was not sure at first if the sound was coming from inside of her, from the building emotion that felt as if she might explode. It wasn't, though. It was her father, calling her, forcing her out so that he could take her blood.

"Circe," Evan insisted.

Her eyes met his. Her feet did not move. "Why does he want me? What is it that I have—what is in my magic that is so much stronger than the others?"

Evan turned her to face him full on. "Your mother was a descendant of the gods. The demon sent to find you could smell it in your blood."

Circe nodded. It made sense. Horrible as it was, this was the sort of thing that called for a curse. This was the sort of magic the aunts would do anything to protect.

The sort of power a mage would kill for.

"Okay," she said to the stairwell door. "I'm ready."

Evan's hand pressed briefly to her back, promising he'd be there for her. She felt his concern, though, as he moved past her to open the door. He did not know the true strength inside her, but he was willing to risk himself anyway.

She followed him down the back stairwell—a covert passage for employees—and beyond her new resolve, she could sense Evan's fear turning to something else. The hex in his blood was colder, the magic not boiling to the surface the way she might have expected but rising nonetheless.

"Evan," she said. "Please don't shift. I will protect you."

He stopped on the landing between the first and second floor, looked up at her where she stood the few steps above him. Circe understood now how Evan's curse was hurting him. How the desire to shift brought it on, and how each shift was slowly draining him. Whatever time Evan had left, she did not want him to waste on her behalf.

She felt the cold settle in him once more, saw his eyes go soft even as his mouth flattened into a grimace. Circe walked past him to the stairwell door.

"I promise," she said. "Just trust in me."

They silently walked into the first-floor lobby, finding the quickest exit from the inn. The moment they were outside, Evan sensed the shifters lingering near the edge of the building. They moved toward Circe and Evan, and Circe could feel the change in him. She put a hand on his arm, felt the hairs raised on his skin. She didn't have to say it again. She had asked him not to shift, and he'd resist it if he could. If the magic would let him.

Circe glared at the approaching men.

"Don't lay a hand on either of us," she said levelly. The men hesitated, but she knew they'd be under orders. "I will go with you, but touch me once and it will be the last thing you ever touch as a man."

Her words were effective. The shifters must have been warned. Circe wondered why all the men her father had sent her were shifters, given her ability. Did he assume she could not transform a man who already shifted? That her power would be less potent? Or was that power a talent she'd been given by him? She wanted to know what he knew about her gift, but she would have to think about that later. She could not let him get inside her head.

Evan put his hand on the small of Circe's back, leading her toward the street. He must have been able to sense more than just the shifters, or somehow the mages had a way to call him to them using his blood. She hoped that wasn't the case. Being tied to one hex was bad enough.

She wanted to ask Evan how powerful her father was, but she knew the answer already. Powerful enough an entire coven of witches was determined to stop him from doing a blood rite. Powerful enough he was able to call her from their room at the inn despite her protections. They walked the few blocks to where the street ended, and Evan kept moving through the low vegetation that led into trees.

They were going to the forest.

The late afternoon sun threw shadows across the ground, but the shadows were not long enough. The equinox had not passed. She tried to remember the words the aunts had used in her yearly rituals, how they might have been trying to protect her. To delay this.

They walked on, the trees tall and thin, leaving Circe feeling exposed and vulnerable. She wrapped her arms around herself, wishing she had worn a coat. Wishing she had filled her pockets with more concoctions than her meager supply. The ground was covered with snow, unlike the areas that had been cleared in town. Circe stepped carefully over the hidden roots and vines. She saw figures moving behind the trees, shapes of men and cloaks and beings that were not the locals of Havenwood Falls.

These were her father's men.

Eventually, they reached a clearing, patches of snow and fallen pine needles over barren ground. Seven mages stood in a semicircle at the far edge of it, hooded cloaks covering their forms. At least ten more figures moved through the trees behind them, but Circe did not know which were mages and which were their hired hands. At their entrance into the clearing, the mages shifted, and Circe saw the stone platform beyond.

She felt the figures moving behind her and Evan, knew they were trying to cage her in.

"I came of my own accord," she announced. Her eyes were on the central figure—not taller or broader than any other man but positioned in the center of power. "I will not be threatened in my own home."

There was no response from the waiting mages. Circe could feel

Evan's tension beside her, his need to shift causing him physical pain.

"I demand that you release the bond on Evan Grey. That you remove yourself from Havenwood Falls and never return."

There. They didn't care, but she'd said it. It made her feel a little better that they'd been warned.

"Evan," Circe said. "Stand behind me."

His gaze snapped to her, disbelief shaping his expression in an almost comical way. Still, she did not remove her attention from her father.

Evan stepped behind her, eyes on the men who inched nearer every second that passed. One of the figures lit two candles on the stone altar, another began to burn smudge sticks, filling the clearing with spice and smoke. The mages began to speak, reciting a low, rhythmic chant in a language unfamiliar to her. She'd waited long enough. They had no intention of hearing her out.

Circe unwound the bracelet at her wrist, crushing its beads in the palm of her hand. She let the dust fall around them, singing the words of the spell loud and clear.

The mages stopped chanting, their cloaked forms going still. A precise wind drove through the clearing, knocking out the candle flames and eating the smoke, pulling the hems of the mages' cloaks to snap in the gust.

Evan murmured his approval behind her, but Circe was frozen. "That wasn't me."

A cackle cut through the now still air, and Circe had to bite down a crazed laugh of her own. *Tia.* It was Tia. Thirteen witches came into the clearing at a full run, and by the sound of things behind her, Circe counted at least three of the shifters down and out.

That still left a few too many for her liking.

The aunts lined the trees behind Circe, fanning out on either side. She could feel Evan's breath on her neck behind her. He'd no longer need to watch her back. Her coven had done that.

More cloaked figures moved from behind the trees, the sounds beyond Circe's and Evan's backs indicating they'd grown to quite a crowd. Circe couldn't look away from her target.

She could not give him even a breath to take advantage.

He had no such concern. His gaze left hers to scan the clearing, to take in those who stood around her.

"She knows, Lucius." The voice came from beside her, unmistakably Morgan's, but the tone chilling in a way Circe had never heard, even counting the time one of Anise's cats had shredded Morgan's favorite black strappy dress.

The man Circe stared at lifted a hand, his flesh covered in black symbols and lines. He drew down his hood. His hair was short and dark, his skin olive, his eyes green. He looked familiar, but not because he was anyone Circe had ever seen. The likeness was in the tilt of his eyes, the shape of his nose. That of a father and daughter. That of the woman in Circe's own mirror.

She hated that they shared anything in common, let alone blood.

He held his hands forward and said in a conversational tone, "Daughter."

Circe felt the bile rise in her throat. She had tried to talk to him, she had stood right before him, and he'd never flinched. And now, ritual candles burned out and smoke cleared away, he would assume she had forgotten. That she would run to his open arms.

She stepped forward, as if to do exactly that.

She felt Evan try to move with her, but one of the aunts must have bade him to stay. She was glad of it. She didn't want him in reach of this man who would sacrifice his own kin.

"I thought you left me," Circe said. "All these years."

His expression did not change, but as she moved closer, she

could see the toll his spells had placed on him. The reason he craved the power so bad.

"I would never leave you," he told her. "You were stolen from my very arms."

There was a rumble of mutters and growls from the witches behind her, but Circe did not turn around. She kept placing one foot in front of the other, moving closer to this man who wanted her dead. "And now," she answered, "here I am."

He took on an air of uncertainty then, sudden and probably something rarely seen.

Circe liked that.

His hands came down, palms facing her. "That's close enough."

She smiled. "Yes," she said. "I believe it is."

Lucius threw his arms wide, and power burst through the clearing. It hurt, nearly knocking her from her feet, but Circe felt the bottle Louisa had dropped in her pocket earlier explode, and she understood that was why she'd been able to withstand the hit. Palms fisted, Circe stared up at this man, no feelings of love for him in her heart. She'd been hurt by them, truly, but the coven behind her was her real family. Her only family.

This man was a monster.

Lucius's fingers drew in, and he used the power to call to Evan. He had Evan's blood; Circe couldn't do anything about that. Still, she stood her ground.

There was a cry behind her, Evan shifting unwillingly into a beast. Circe could not help him. She could not turn around. It sounded as if his bones were breaking, as if his body was being torn to shreds. But the magic would put him back together. The hex inside of him would keep him alive. Moments passed, and then she could feel him, moving toward her until his ragged breath whispered up the back of her neck and the fur of his muzzle brushed her skin.

"You would have him eat me, then?"

Her father stared at her. All he needed was her blood on that altar by 3:58 p.m. He did not care how it got there.

She felt the tear trickle over the curve of her cheek. She did not need to fake that, but the sentiment was not for her father. It was for Evan. Circe couldn't imagine the pain he must be in—being forced into his beast form by first a witch's hex, and now by this mage. She used the grief anyway, as if she might raise her hand to wipe those tears. When her fisted hands reached high enough, she turned them open, palm up, and blew the remaining dust into her father's face.

The line of mages sprang forward, shouting words of power and throwing castings of their own. But it was too late. Circe spat, leapt forward to brace her hands on her father—on the exposed flesh of his neck and face. Cloaked figures filled the clearing, throwing the mages to the ground with their powers and their bare hands. A chorus of howls echoed through the trees, both animal and man, but Circe could not focus on anything but the task before her, this one thing that was the hardest spell she'd ever cast.

She could feel Lucius's energy fighting her, and it only made her push back harder. She thrust her magic into him. Circe did not need his blood. She had power of her own, the very thing he'd wanted to steal, and she could feel it growing every moment closer to the equinox. The aunts' ritual had not been performed. Circe's power had never been stronger.

Lucius writhed and struggled beneath her, snapping his jaws and digging his clawed fingers into the earth. Darkness shot through his veins, crossing the tattoos in hectic patterns. His hands began to lengthen, his skin turning ashen before sprouting coarse black fur. She had never done an animal she was unfamiliar with, and her lack of remembered details and anger were turning him more monstrous than she might have intended. She yanked the cord of his cloak free of the material and bound him where he lay, this once-deadly mage now panting and hopeless and utterly beaten by a single measly witch.

Circe smiled, standing to dust her palms off on her pant legs. Morgan came beside her, staring down at the dark, mangled form. She shook her head. "Oh, Circe."

Circe looked up at her, for Morgan was quite tall when she wanted to be. "What?" she said. "Isn't that what you wanted?"

Tia popped up on her other side, snorted a laugh. "Men are pigs and all?"

She was trying out that sarcasm thing; Circe thought she liked it.

"Technically a boar, I think." She shrugged, turned to survey the clearing. Six cloaked mages scattered the ground, beaten and bloodied to various degrees, all bound with spelled twine or leathers, all gagged with their own cloaks to prevent spellcasting. Three cloaked figures neared, dropping their hoods.

"Addie," Circe breathed.

Addie gave Circe a nod and kicked her black boots against a stone to knock the snow loose. "Nice job, C."

"Circe," Morgan said, gesturing to the silver-haired woman beside Addie and a tall man with slick black hair farther out. "This is Saundra Beaumont and Roman Bishop."

Saundra nodded, but instead of a *hey* gesture like Addie's, this one clearly meant business. The man glanced at her, his blue eyes interested but his demeanor leaning more toward bored or annoyed, which one Circe couldn't be sure.

Circe looked to Morgan.

"Both sit on the Court of the Sun and the Moon and on the High Council of the Luna Coven," Morgan explained. "Saundra is Lyra's mother. She and Roman agreed to assist with your situation in exchange for a bit of help from us. Lucius, you see, was more than a danger to only you. He worked for an exceptionally nasty entity known as the Collector. They will take custody of Lucius, and he will no longer be a threat to us."

"The Collector?" Circe asked.

"That's not for you to worry about," Morgan assured her. "The important thing is that Lucius has been handled, and what he planned to do to you and, eventually, other residents of Havenwood Falls, will never come to pass."

Circe blinked, glancing around the clearing again. The cloaked figures were dissipating. Roman gestured loosely to Lucius's body, bound as it was. "Take him to the cell."

There was more movement as cloaked figures heeded his order, and Saundra gave Morgan a significant look. Circe paid the ordeal no attention—she had no interest in where they took that man who had been nothing like a father. Instead, she reached into her back pocket, drawing free the tarot card she'd received at the festival.

She presented it to Morgan, letting the printed accusation speak for itself.

Morgan cleared her throat. "Yes, dear. Perhaps we should discuss this later, privately."

Circe crossed her arms, stood her ground. She was done with this, and even if she didn't know much about who this Saundra and Roman were to Morgan, she was done waiting. "How about now?"

Morgan sighed, sliding the card into the folds of her cloak. "The protections we laid on you—your curse, as you have come to know it—was never the true cause of your doom. Your future had been foretold long before you came to us, and as such, we had no choice but to take action. It is true that your mother faced her own end due to a curse, but only after she fell into Lucius's hands. That was when the darkness took her."

At Circe's flinch, Morgan placed a hand over hers. "We saved you, Circe. Protected you in the only way we knew how."

Circe nodded for her to go on.

Morgan pressed her lips together, and Circe could tell she avoided glancing at Saundra and Roman, who watched on. She said, "Prophecy said your fate would come when you created a bond with a shifter, someone with dirty blood that Lucius would be able to track back to you. So we did what we could to delay that end. To keep them from finding you. Unfortunately, Lucius did what he could as well."

"And the rituals?" Circe asked.

Morgan's hand went to Circe's cheek. "We fell in love with you the moment we laid eyes on you, child. We could have done nothing else but everything in our power to save you."

Circe drew a breath, trying to keep the pain in her chest from showing. She stepped back from Morgan so that her aunt might not see. She didn't want to relive those memories now, not in front of everyone.

Not in front of anyone.

She watched as Roman drew up the hood of his cloak and turned, Saundra following after. Addie gave Circe a small smile. Circe had a feeling none of this was as new to them as it was to her.

She took in the clearing again. She did not see the shifters Lucius had had control of. She did not know how much of this battle she had missed, but as she scanned the forest, she could not focus on the rest any longer.

She could only see Evan.

Anise and Louisa squatted over him, Hazel standing behind them with her hands bent into unnatural shapes. Like a puppet master.

"Let him go," Circe said.

"We're only keeping him safe. We didn't want him to harm you."

Circe moved toward the group. "He can't hurt me now. Lucius

is no longer a man—he can only use Evan's blood when he's in human form."

Anise raised a speculative brow.

"I just know," Circe told her. She waved her hands to shoo them away.

The aunts watched her watch Evan, muttering and whispering amongst themselves.

"I thought this curse was supposed to keep her away from men . . . looks like he got his hooks in her anyway, doesn't it? I told you he'd follow her here . . . that's how those prophecies work, you can't trust them . . . every single time. You just can't win . . . maybe we should have used nightsbane . . . would you stop with the drugging everyone all the time, did you ever consider maybe that's not the answer . . ."

Evan was bleeding through large patches of matted fur. He was gray all over, dark streaked with ash. His arms were long, nearly the length of his back legs. His feet were like a jungle cat's, but the rest of him resembled something large and canine. He was still his full size, only stretched into something terrible and lethal and covered with hair. She knelt beside him, placed a hand on his fur where his shoulder might be. He did not move, but his eyes opened, black and depthless, to look at her.

"I'm here, Evan."

He blinked, the sound that came out of him half whine, half growl. The shift on its own would have been bad enough. At Lucius's hand, it must have been a thousand times worse.

Circe looked up at the aunts. "Did Lucius give this power to me? Is that man the reason I can do what I do?"

Louisa's eyes were soft, but her voice rang strong and true. "No. Nothing that is good in you came from that man. Your mother gave you this gift, and that's what it is. That thief could not do it on his own. He was only obsessed with those who could."

81

"And the lies, they're done now?"

Anise winced. "It was only to help you, dear. Only to keep you safe."

Circe thought of the rituals she'd grown up with. The fears they'd instilled in her.

The curse they'd warned her was to bring her end.

She stroked the suffering beast with a trembling hand, so sorry that she'd ever been such a fool.

"I'll help you, Evan." She glanced over his wounded form and felt the cold hex beneath his skin. "I don't know how, but I'll help you."

EPILOGUE

*C*irce sat at her studio desk, staring at the calendar pinned above it on her apartment wall. She'd been painting, working on a watercolor sketch of the shops on Main Street, some of her favorite places to be. The washed-out figures of locals walked in front of Shelf Indulgence's imaginative window display and sat on a bench outside Madame Tahini's Potions, Lotions, Palm Readings, and Other Extra-Sensory Services. They made their way into Coffee Haven for tea and art, two of Circe's favorite things of all.

She smiled as she dropped her brush into the glass jar she'd picked up at Howe's Herbal Shoppe, thinking of how she might approach Willow Fairchild—the empath she'd since discovered was fae and the owner of Coffee Haven—with her newly finished watercolor in hand. Havenwood Falls was full of artists, and Circe felt the peculiar nervous excitement of sharing her art with peers. She had been nothing but happy the last few months, and more often than ever in her life she forgot to watch the time go by. Without a countdown to the day her curse would commence, dates escaped her notice, slipped by as if they were nothing at all.

But now she'd noticed. Today was June twenty-first, the summer solstice, and it could not help but bring to mind that first day of spring. The aunts had told her more truths after all, that Tia had been warned in prophecy, that Anise had read it in her leaves, that Louisa had thrown the prediction in bones. Some terrible and epic thing was bound to happen, and the only way to save Circe was to hide her from her own goddess blood. To create a curse that would bind her, that would bring her up and direct her here, where a slim few survivable outcomes awaited her instead of the thousand other nasty ends. Her blood had been so powerful, they'd been forced to rebind the magic every spring.

To hide her from the mages. From her father.

They hadn't counted on Evan, though. The hex in his blood was not what they'd expected from a shifter, and they'd had enough trouble getting rid of him that they knew they were running out of time. Circe's fate was coming.

When the Court had discovered Lucius had a connection to the Collector, Saundra had sent Lyra right away. She'd known that Lucius was Circe's father, and so they removed the aunts' memory blocks and together made a plan to bring Circe to the safety of Havenwood Falls. To trap Lucius before he could gain the power he needed to continue the Collector's schemes.

The aunts explained they had made arrangements with the Luna Coven and the Court of the Sun and the Moon for the day of the ritual, that each had been there in case Circe had needed them, but that the aunts had had faith she would do the right thing. That she could take care of herself. They'd insisted she go to the festival that day so that she might be under the protection of the locals during Lucius's planned ritual. And so that she could face her father before the Court took custody of him. Plus, Anise had said, they just really loved festivals.

Circe had finally forgiven the aunts, but she'd refused to follow them back to the church where she'd been raised. Havenwood Falls was her home now, and despite what they thought of its weather and Evan's presence here, Havenwood Falls was where she intended to stay. Hazel had hugged her and whispered that the cold was certainly worth it in exchange for the view. Circe was still not sure if Hazel had meant the view of the mountains or the view that was Evan, but she'd wished them well and sent them on their way, with permission to arrange visits only when invited by Circe.

You had to be strict with witches.

She'd also discovered that not only had the Court of the Sun and the Moon known of the aunts' plot all along, they were the reason Lucius and his mages had made it past the town wards. Lucius had a history that Circe knew little about, but apparently he'd done enough to warrant letting him believe he'd found a way to circumvent their protections so they could be done with him once and for all.

Who the Collector was, Circe didn't think she'd ever know. The Court went above and beyond to protect its borders, and no matter what their own stake in it, Circe would be forever grateful for what they'd done for her. She didn't care how they'd dealt with Lucius once he'd been taken from that clearing, and she wasn't sure she ever wanted to find out. But she hoped someday she could be more like the members of the Court, that she might learn how to better use her power to help the Havenwood Falls residents the way she'd been helping Evan.

It was a beautiful possibility, the idea of turning something that had been a curse into good. What she'd done for Evan, maybe she could do for others. She had a satisfying job at the animal hospital, and she was meeting so many locals and supernaturals, she had more than just hope.

Circe was discovering that maybe she wasn't such an introvert after all. Maybe she just hadn't found her people before.

There was still the issue of figuring out how to remove Evan's hex, to clean his blood from both its ties to that sorceress and to Circe's father, but her magic could at least give him a reprieve. She could at least slow the process until something more could be done.

She could give him a chance at life.

Circe glanced at the *jump* tattooed on her ring finger, remembering the quote. *Go to the edge of the cliff and jump off. Build your wings on the way down.* Evan had received his Court-issued tattoo from Addie days after Circe had returned him to his human form. It was small and clean, covering the scar the mages had left at the base of his thumb. *Wings*, it read. Evan had gotten a tattoo of wings. She recalled the first time she'd seen it, the blush on his skin and the thrill in her heart.

It gave her butterflies even now.

Circe glanced at the clock, remembering the date was important for something else. Evan was at work until five, finally able to hold a steady job now that he could mostly contain his shifting. McCabe & Sons Construction had hired him as a trial for the summer, as soon as business had picked up after the spring thaw. The McCabes were shifters, and they understood Evan's condition. If he were to have a slip, Circe knew they would have his back—even if Evan hadn't seemed to take to the cat shifters as quickly as he had some of the other locals.

They had both found their footing here. They had begun to make friends, to feel anchored.

To look forward without fear.

Evan had an apartment of his own now in Havenwood Village, and he would be knocking on her door by six sharp. The summer solstice brought another festival on the square: Midsummer's Night. Circe had never been so eager for a fair, but this one would be especially remarkable. The human residents of Havenwood Falls would be put into a deep sleep, so that the supernatural beings who filled the town could have a night free to be their true selves. Evan's curse would allow him to attend, and the night would be filled with games and dancing, and the mayhem that only supernaturals were capable of. She smiled at the thought of it, at the anticipation of spending it with Evan, and some part of her, far in the back of her mind, knew that if it went well, she might even someday invite the aunts.

～

Song of the Witches
by
William Shakespeare
From Macbeth, Act IV, Scene 1

Round about the cauldron go:
In the poisoned entrails throw.
Toad, that under cold stone
Days and nights has thirty-one
Sweated venom sleeping got,
Boil thou first i' the charmed pot.

Double, double toil and trouble;
Fire burn and cauldron bubble.

Fillet of a fenny snake,
In the cauldron boil and bake;
Eye of newt and toe of frog,
Wool of bat and tongue of dog,
Adder's fork and blind-worm's sting,
Lizard's leg and owlet's wing.
For a charm of powerful trouble,

Like a hell-broth boil and bubble.

Double, double toil and trouble;
Fire burn and cauldron bubble.

Scale of dragon, tooth of wolf,
Witch's mummy, maw and gulf
Of the ravin'd salt-sea shark,
Root of hemlock digg'd i' the dark,
Liver of blaspheming Jew;
Gall of goat; and slips of yew
Sliver'd in the moon's eclipse;
Nose of Turk, and Tartar's lips;
Finger of birth-strangled babe
Ditch-deliver'd by a drab,
Make the gruel thick and slab:
Add thereto a tiger's chaudron,
For the ingredients of our cauldron.

Double, double toil and trouble,
Fire burn and cauldron bubble.
Cool it with a baboon's blood,
Then the charm is firm and good.

We hope you enjoyed this story in the Havenwood Falls series
featuring a variety of supernatural creatures. The series is a
collaborative effort by multiple authors. You might also enjoy these
stories:
Forget You Not, Lose You Not and Break Me Not by Kristie Cook
Ink & Fire by R.K. Ryals

Also look for the YA line, Havenwood Falls High; the historical paranormal line, Legends of Havenwood Falls; the sexier side of town, Havenwood Falls Sin & Silk; the local supernatural college, Sun & Moon Academy; and the Havenwood Falls holiday short story anthologies.

Stay up to date at www.HavenwoodFalls.com

ABOUT THE AUTHOR

Melissa is the author of ten YA and fantasy novels, and countless to-do lists. She is currently working on the next book, but when not writing can generally be found talking (about books), painting (things she's read in books), or hiding between her headphones (listening to books). Check out her Instagram for art and book love or follow via one of the many links at www.melissa-wright.com

For info on contests and new releases, sign up for the newsletter here: http://eepurl.com/zbisj

ACKNOWLEDGMENTS

Thank you Kristie Cook for allowing me to have some small part in the Havenwood Falls world and its community of amazing authors. This has been an adventure of the best kind. Thanks to each of the Havenwood Falls authors for welcoming me, and for sharing your creations so graciously. Special thanks to author E.J. Fechenda for the use of her characters at Coffee Haven and McCabe & Sons Construction (and for giving poor Evan a job), Kristie Cook for a room at Whisper Falls Inn, and for Addie and the Court, to Lila Felix for serving the tacos, Randi Cooley Wilson for Callie, and R.K. Ryals for fortunes and music with Eloise at the Into the Mystic New Age and Psychic Fair, and for Isa Hilton and Cressida Manos at the Havenwood Falls Animal Hospital and shelter. Thank you to all the Havenwood Falls authors who've dreamed up a world so wonderful and allowed me to play in it. Thanks to my crit partner Jennifer Silverwood for keeping me in line. Thank you to the incredible Ang'dora Productions team, the amazing beta readers and editors, and to designer Regina Wamba for the beautiful cover art.

AN EXCERPT

~ A Havenwood Falls New Adult Novella ~

HAVENWOOD FALLS

OF SALT AND STARS

SEVEN JANE

Of Salt and Stars (A Havenwood Falls Novella) by Seven Jane

Two women, one love, and a curse lurking in deep, dark waters.

For as long as she can remember, Maris Heilen has been haunted by dreams of a beautiful woman beckoning to her from beneath the water. These dreams have been Maris's only constant. She's lived her life like a leaf caught in the rushing tide: no rules, no commitments, and no long-term lovers, either—just a string of broken hearts that have tried to anchor her unwilling heart to the earth. When her dreams take on a new sense of urgency following the mysterious death of her estranged father, Maris knows it's time to uproot and keep moving, her soul pulled to the west, toward the water—toward *her*.

Instead Maris finds herself drawn to a surreal little town high in the Colorado mountains, where she begins to believe her dream might be much closer to reality than she'd ever imagined. When she discovers her past is linked to a legend even more haunting than her dreams—and that the woman in them is not only real but in danger of being lost to an unfathomable darkness—Maris resolves to outshine the evil that has crept into a small corner of a forgotten forest in Havenwood Falls.

OF SALT AND STARS

BY SEVEN JANE

MANY YEARS AGO

At the edge of the lush green forests that surround Havenwood Falls, where the sweet-smelling junipers and majestic pines tickle the walls of the silver snowcapped mountains that border the town, in a place seldom traveled and even less often remembered, there once stood a well.

It was a well of the wishing sort, with a peaked cedar canopy that hovered above a yawning mouth of gray stone rendered soft by the breath of innumerable years. The well was one of those rare structures that during the day appeared carved of sunlight, its golden shine so blinding that the only way to look upon it was to shield one's eyes and sip it in quick glances lest it steal your vision completely. At night, however, the well was perhaps even more beautiful, when under the glow of a silver moon it seemed as soft and elusive as the stuff of dreams, formed into being by the twinkling of a thousand stars. Regardless of the time of day, the air always seemed more fragrant near the well—scented by day with a pomander of wildflowers and by night with the heady flora of thistle and night-blooming jasmine. So tangible, too, was the magic in this place that the air was always just a little cooler here—a wrap was necessary even during the hottest parts of the year—and it was so quiet that the whisper of the clear water that swelled nearly to the well's lips could even be heard above the rustling of the forest itself.

The animals that lived in the surrounding wood did not drink from the well, nor was its water harvested as drinking water for the town. Indeed, no bucket was ever hung from the awning from which to draw, for those few who knew of the well also knew that it was enchanted, and its waters imbued with a very special sort of magic. See, the well was not merely the fount of a spring. Far below the water's surface, in a hidden lake in a cavern below the earth, dwelled a creature as temporal and beautiful as the structure itself—a naiad by the name Noelani.

The naiad's well was a carefully guarded secret in Havenwood Falls, and only a few knew of its location, but those that were lucky enough to know the well's secret—most often women but occasionally men and children as well—would visit. There they would cut their hair and cast hushed wishes to Noelani, the Lady of the Water, and dip long wooden spoons into the well for a sip of her water's magic.

Most of the well's patrons—both human and supernatural alike —wished for love, for like other naiads, Noelani was a spirit of such things. Young girls were keen to look for their beloved's reflection hovering under the wildflower petals that floated on the well's surface. Older—but no less lovestruck—young brides garbed in their wedding dresses came to collect vials of Noelani's water, which brought them fertility. And when their bones began to ache, elderly women in their widow's habits sipped spoonsful of the well's water for vitality. If one was lucky, they might even catch a glimpse of the naiad herself, alight on the well's brim under the glow of the sun or the full moon, her long red hair swirling in the water beneath her as she sang songs more beautiful than those of the sirens at the banks of the waterfalls on the other side of Havenwood Falls. If this were the case, then the person would have been even more richly blessed, for it was said that whoever's eyes met Noelani's would be granted the gift of her magic, and some of her love would remain in their hearts forever, making all of their days blessed and sweet.

For many years, the naiad's well was a place of good fortune for all who visited. Noelani was happy, and her water was pure. But that was long ago, and such lovely places rarely endure for long— even those so consumed with love, for love is the most fickle of all beasts.

The opposite of love is not hate but jealousy, and it was this that caused the well to ferment and the magic of Noelani to become diseased. It was jealousy of the ugliest kind—that which bleeds from the eyes and can sour milk just by the look of it—that led to the death of a young bride by the name of Stella Malley, who, on the very eve of her wedding, had come to ask the naiad's blessing and instead found herself drowned by the man who'd promised to marry her.

The manner in which he killed her—some say he held her head below the water until her lungs filled all the way to her throat, others that he strangled her with the train of her veil and sank her body with stones—is less important than his reason for doing so. The root of his this man's darkness was jealousy, not of what he couldn't have—for Stella had promised to be his—but of what he couldn't *control*. With her long black hair, creamed honey skin, and black eyes that sparkled like stars, Stella was as lovely as the midnight sky. But even more charming than her face was her heart, which drew others to her in droves and caused her to outshine the man who would have been her husband, and—had such a thing been possible—her shadow.

The man—his name important only because it is on the list of those that have been banished from Havenwood Falls, and such things are sparingly done—was a Mister Paul Heilen. And when Heilen forced his betrothed's face into the naiad's well, Noelani watched, helpless from below as Stella thrashed, the poor girl's lungs filling with water she could not breathe. As precious moments passed, Noelani saw the light inside Stella's eyes grow dim and faint until it burnt out altogether, and when the richness of her skin had been replaced with the gray tinge of death, her face relaxed and her mouth fell open.

Only Noelani heard Stella's final scream, and the sound was so anguished that when it infused the water, it also filled the naiad's heart with rage. With Stella's scream in her stomach, the naiad shrieked, her beautiful voice so racked with pain that when it broke forth from the water, the drops pierced Heilen's skin like shards of glass, causing him to stumble and look into the well. When he did, his eyes met Noelani's. He saw her red hair pooled like blood around her and her pearly white teeth grown long with fury, and he was afraid. And as the jealous are also often cowards, he ran, leaving Stella's body to topple into the well and sink, lost forever.

By the time Stella's corpse had made its way to the bottom of the well, it had turned the blue water black, and along with it, Noelani's heart. Death is a sorrowful thing, but murder is bitter, and crimes of passion are tinged with powerful dark magic that can snuff out even the brightest candle. Noelani's warmth turned cold as stone within her, and the love inside her drowned in a pool of darkness much in the same way that Stella Malley had been drowned in Heilen's.

Still, Noelani had seen the face of the man who'd murdered his bride, and so when he left the naiad's well, a part of her had been forced to go with him, trapped inside his eyes. The love held within Noelani's magic soon soured within him, turning every drop of love he encountered into something vapid and impenetrable until, one night many years later, he drowned in his bed where he slept—as dry and far from the water as he had been able to go to escape what he'd seen that night in the well. Heilen's death was a mystery, for how could a man as dry as a dead leaf choke on water that had risen up his throat from his own insides? But the doctors said he had drowned, and so he had. And because of the curse Heilen had brought upon himself and Noelani, there had been no one left behind to mourn his death, for he had never again had the chance for love.

Time has changed the well. What was once a place of love and light has fallen largely to the ruin of legend. Years have passed since any girl or young bride or even a widow has dared visit its part of the forest, for they know there is no love left for the naiad to give. The well's once clear and flowing water has sunk lower and lower until all that remains at the bottom is salt from Noelani's tears. The cool air around the well has iced over, the remnants of Noelani's sobs still on the air in the form of ice and frost, and the forest has crept in around the well until the meadow has been overcome completely by a rambling snarl of thorn and root. The scent of wildflowers has been overrun by the stench of death, and in the absence of Noelani's light, the forest had grown thick with loveless creatures both cruel and vile.

None has seen the naiad Noelani, but those who tell tales of such things insist that Stella's bitter death consumed the once lovely creature, her beautiful red hair turned black, and her skin grew gaunt and pallid like a corpse left too long underwater. Those who might wander too far into the woods are warned to avoid the wrath of the well, for even if one were to survive the dangers of the forest, the creature that would crawl forth from her prison would not be the naiad, but a miserable and cursed thing. A rusalka they called Noelani now—a monster, dark and sinister, with a heart consumed with spiteful evil. And if she saw you, it would not be blessing that she'd give. Instead, she would pass on her curse and drag you down into the depths of darkness with her.

The time of the well has passed, and the love of Noelani is lost. What remained of her magic passed to Heilen, and when he died, it faded with him—or so those who remember were inclined to believe. Noelani's story has faded largely to legend, and whatever remains of her—whether naiad or rusalka—is left to wallow in her well, guarded by the Court of the Sun and the Moon, who leave Noelani in peace so long as she brings no harm to the residents of Havenwood Falls. Some once whispered of a cure, a return of Noelani's love that could only be brought about from the seeds of her deepest hate, but it has been many years, and none have come forward that might break her curse and heal her broken heart.

And so Noelani waits, trapped in her own darkness, for a star to save her.

PRESENT DAY

Maris's eyes snapped open in the midnight darkness of her bedroom. She'd been having that dream again—the same one she'd been having her whole life. Okay, well, maybe not her *whole* life, but certainly for as many of her twenty-four years as she could remember. For the most part, they'd been the passing kind of nighttime fancies, the type that you woke up still feeling but only barely able to remember, and even those last little tendrils had faded completely by the time her feet touched the morning floor. But lately, the dreams had begun to linger, growing more and more insistent, as if they were trying to tell her something—to carve the memory of them into her heart with ghostly fingers and bedtime secrets. And they had begun to hurt, as if the longing in her dreams was enough to wound her heart, so that Maris sometimes woke with a dull ache in her chest.

Lately, her awakenings had grown even stranger. Sometimes she woke with her mouth full of warm, salty water. Other times she'd find strands of hair much darker than her own wound in the crevices of her body—around the backs of knees, her wrists, her throat—but when she'd go to remove them the strands would be gone. At first it had baffled and confused her, and lately it began to frighten her, although it was impossible to say why because it was impossible to understand in the first place.

This bramble stuck in Maris's daytime thoughts, invading her dreams night after night in a pattern that had become as regular as her heartbeat. After Maris's father passed away a little more than a month ago—dried up and dead broke in some pitiful little hostel somewhere in the desert while she'd been buried under snow in Denver—the dreams had taken on an air of urgency, and the strange incidents had increased. Still, even though she often woke up sweat-drenched and panting, Maris could barely remember the dream by the time her eyes opened, and certainly couldn't recall enough to decipher any hidden message.

Insofar as she could tell, there was nothing truly remarkable about the dream itself. There was no grand inspiration or message that could be decoded with a dream dictionary, and she'd never once experienced any of that waking form of déjà vu that might connect the dream to her real life. The strange events aside, the dream wasn't scary or suspenseful—at least not enough that she would remember it being so. It wasn't even particularly thrilling. In fact, it was much the opposite. The scraps she could remember were beautiful—maybe *the* most beautiful she'd ever had, like something out of a fairy tale.

In the dream, it was always light out, but only just barely, with wisps of sunset coloring the sky in pastel shades of pink and orange. There was a forest she'd never set foot in and a small pool of water she'd never swum in, and both of these were more lush and vibrant than any parcel of land she'd ever seen—even in Colorado, where beautiful landscapes were a dime a dozen. But even more breathtaking than the scenery, there was *her*.

The woman in the dream.

The woman *of* her dreams.

The woman in Maris's dream was always constant, even if the scenery changed—which it did, but only with the weather, which followed the seasonal cycle of Maris's waking life. The woman—if she was that, because there was something distinctly magical about her that marked her as not completely human but certainly feminine—swam in a large stone well. Sometimes the water that rippled atop the edges of the stones was frosted over with a layer of glittering ice; other times Maris could tell by its look that it was as warm as bathwater. Throughout all of these, however, the woman never changed. She always appeared, rising out of the water so that it spilled off her milk-white skin like rain and weighed down hair that was the color of liquid scarlet but might have been strawberry blond when dry. She had the most dazzling emerald-green eyes and a curve to her lips that was simultaneously taunting and coy, and she never wore anything more than a thin white slip of a dress, which gave her an air of innocence that was almost certainly misleading if one judged the way it clung, damp and revealing, against her flesh. She seemed always covered in dew and softness, and there was a small mark on the inside of one of her wrists: a tattoo of a star with four lines that stretched to create eight points —the one called the North Star.

"Maris," the woman would whisper, her lips shiny and wet with water and a voice that sounded like the ocean and deeper things and had a way of pulling Maris's heart into her throat.

"Yes," Maris would hear herself responding, as in her peripheral vision she watched her own hand reach for the water—for the woman in the water.

"Come away with me," the woman would say then, and the words were nectar on Maris's tongue when at last she closed the distance between the two of them and could taste the words on the woman's waiting lips. There was something that changed in Maris each time she kissed the woman in the well—a blossoming inside of her that grew and became more solid and real every time she touched the woman's lips with hers, until the dream had ceased to be a fantasy and began to feel like home.

If Maris had her way, she'd wrap every bit of herself—every strand of her dishwater blond hair, every square inch of the freckled, sun-kissed skin she'd inherited from the mother she'd never known, each of her ten long fingers and ten agile toes— around the woman in her dream. She'd hold her close, touch her lips against her sweet, glistening flesh, and slide with her beneath the water and never let her go. But then, just as this seemed like it might be a possibility, the dream would end, and Maris's eyes would open somewhere grim and dry and far away, the ethereal image of the woman's eyes tinting her vision emerald until she blinked it away. Darkness would creep in on the edges of the dream, and all would be lost—until the next night.

The woman in the dream had a way of undoing Maris, and not the least of it was because she was a *woman*.

Though she'd often been accused of being insatiable when it came to matters of the heart—a trait she'd had since puberty and had long since quit being ashamed of—Maris Heilen had never been terribly choosy about her lovers' genders. That wasn't to say she'd been particularly inclusive in her bedroom either, though whether that was by default or decision she wasn't sure. Honestly, the sex of her lovers had always paled in comparison to the actual act itself. Although her tastes had been diverse and far-ranging, her lovers had always and consistently been men. She'd bedded men with blond hair and with dark, men lean and bulky, those fair-skinned and those carved from ebony, tattooed and pierced and unadorned, smooth-faced and bearded, a decade older or a handful of years younger, and every possible combination in between. None had ever held her fancy for very long, though one summer she'd very nearly accidentally fallen for a Frenchman who'd had *chocolat* brown eyes and curling chestnut hair and who didn't speak a lick of English—something that had never been a problem for Maris when weighed against his gentle caresses and endlessly generous lovemaking.

In any case, no matter how many or how different the men that passed through Maris's bed, she was inevitably left unsatisfied, as if there was a hole deep inside of her that could never be filled, though she'd tried like hell to address that in the most literal of ways—not that she'd bothered herself to keep a tally of her conquests. A man wouldn't have done so, so why should she?

And through all of these men, Maris stayed empty, longing for something more that she could never quite articulate, let alone hold in her hands, until at last she'd come to believe it would never be a man who claimed her heart. Even so, Maris had never considered herself to be particularly attracted to women. But, if that was true, then so was the fact that she wasn't *not* attracted to women, either. They were beautiful and so lovely in ways that men just couldn't be, with their long smooth limbs and shapely curves, their soft blushing skin. It had simply never occurred to Maris to take one to bed, and she wasn't sure whether that was disinterest or some sort of deep insecurity—like if she finally opened herself up to someone she might fall into them, never to resurface. Lust, Maris was comfortable with. Lust she could control; she could embrace or let go and it wouldn't hurt her. Love was something else entirely. It was deep and bottomless, consuming.

To love someone, Maris feared, was to drown, and in that sea of emotions, she had never even learned how to swim.

Still, Maris couldn't deny that she felt something stirring within her whenever she caught herself looking at other women in the manner that she often caught men looking at her—all hungry-eyed and wet-lipped, like they were starving creatures just presented with a savory meal. Whatever it was that she felt, Maris had never done more than look, though no woman who had ever crossed Maris's line of sight could have compared to the woman in her dreams, including her *boyfriend*—a word Maris still wasn't entirely comfortable with two years into their relationship—who was currently asleep and snoring softly in the bed beside her.

Barely three months ago Maris had done something she thought she never would, not that she'd ever planned to find herself landlocked in Colorado to begin with. She'd agreed to relieve herself of her private little sanctuary in Lower Highland—a recent addition to Denver's neighborhoods known as one of *the* hippest new neighborhoods in the country—and shack up with a tech nerd from Capitol Hill. Not just any man, but Graham, her current long-term boyfriend who seemed to be becoming a little bit more serious about their relationship than Maris was totally equipped to deal with. Graham, with his unruly jet-black hair and rugged jawline. Graham, who knew how to wear a starched white dress shirt like it was lingerie, and often did, accessorizing his look with the top three buttons left undone under a shadow of dark stubble that had as much of a strange, weakening effect on Maris's knees now as it had on the first night they'd met. It had been the first thing she'd noticed about him when they crossed glances across the bar where she'd been slinging drinks for some extra cash: his unkempt hair and unshaven face juxtaposed against the stark white crispness of his shirt, a brooding counterfeit of a budding businessman. And Graham had not disappointed when Maris had given the last call and the pair had stumbled their way back between the sheets at her place.

Once upon a time, Maris would have taken Graham for a night, maybe two—three if the days bled together, which they often did—and then set him free to float away on the current of her spent desire. Such days, Maris reflected, seemed a lifetime ago now. Two years had a way of feeling like an eternity, and Maris wasn't entirely sure how she felt about anything so endlessly *long* and boringly predictable. She'd always been a free spirit, as restless as the tide itself, and now she felt stuck, like someone had built a dam around her heart and refused to set her free.

Maris's friends said she was settling for Graham, not because he wasn't handsome or stable or all the right things a man approaching thirty should be, but because he *was* handsome and stable and all the right things a man approaching thirty should be. And Maris would never admit it, but she knew she'd only settled for Graham. From his dark hair to his maddening tendency to root his feet in the ground and gather mud around them, Graham was unyielding and inflexible and aggravatingly *planted*. It was what had caused her to give Graham the nickname Grim, though she rarely called him that to his face. What Maris wanted—what she longed for—was the woman she'd been falling in love with in her dreams for the better part of two decades. She wanted to be *free*, as free as she felt in her dreams, where her ladylove waited for her.

Free like the water itself—fluid, flowing, and wavering.

"Come away with me," the woman in her dreams called, and Maris was desperate to go. This desire was bizarre and engrossing and endlessly frustrating, and the need to find this woman was so strong that it kept her constantly on her toes, afraid to settle and ever unsure of where to go. Maris was haunted by it.

But then, Maris had always been haunted, she reflected, her eyes staring at the expanse of ceiling above her head as she waited patiently to fall back asleep. Her father had, too, though he'd never spoken a word of it to his daughter. He hadn't had to. Maris could see it behind his eyes, a constant shadow of some unseen thing that waited for him just beyond the edges of his vision. She'd been able to assemble bits and pieces of his past, but much of the information was confusing and contradictory, like he himself was an unreliable witness. He spoke of a woman, whose face he couldn't remember, lost in a place he wasn't sure existed on any map, and he had insisted more than once these images followed him throughout his dreams in a series of nightmares that always ended with his own death. The last time they spoke, Maris confided her dreams to her father. In turn, he had warned her not to engage with the woman in the well, for it would only bring suffering on her, too. A week later, he died.

Maris's body must have reacted to the tense thoughts invading her mind, because next to her Graham's heavy arm slid reassuringly over her stomach, folding securely between her flesh and the mattress as he brought her body against his. It was an automatic gesture, and Maris allowed herself to be pulled into his gravity on the other side of the bed. She felt the tickle of his dark hair against her skin as he tucked his face into her neck and gently kissed her throat.

"Hey, babe," Graham murmured in a voice thick with sleep.

Something inside her stirred—a need to feel wanted, to feel loved—and the force of it only served to amplify the echoing hollowness in her chest.

"Go back to sleep," Maris whispered as softly as she could, smoothing away his hair.

Part of her wanted to wake Graham up, to pull the sheet away from his body so that the moonlight striped his bare chest and call him into her, but she didn't. With the woman's face still floating up in her memory, such a thing felt cheap and unfair. Instead, Maris let her body melt in the warmth Graham's kiss had left on her neck, hoping it would draw her back to sleep. She put her hand on top of his where it rested heavily against her stomach, forcing herself to reflect on the solidness of Graham's hard body around hers, his skin warm and inviting. It was too dark in the bedroom to see his arm where it lay across her body, but she knew from memory what it would look like—taut, tanned flesh against the stark white of the bed sheets. Graham was comfortable, and safe, but he was also an anchor, and the weight of him made it hard for Maris to breathe. She'd been with him for two years—longer than she'd been with anyone—and every day that passed had only made her sure of one thing.

It's time. The thought bubbled up from the bottom of Maris's thoughts and hung unspoken in the dark bedroom. Behind it came two more words, but these last were not Maris's. They belonged to the woman in the well, and they were sweet and sad and so full of longing that Maris felt a tear slip down her cheek as sleep finally reclaimed her.

"Find me," the woman was calling, and Maris was ready to go.

Purchase *Of Salt and Stars* where books are sold.